T
IS FOR
TIME TRAVEL

A COLLECTION OF TIMELY
SHORT STORIES

STANLEI BELLAN

IS FOR TIME TRAVEL

A COLLECTION OF TIMELY
SHORT STORIES

imagilore
PUBLISHING

T Is for Time Travel
A collection of timely short stories

Copyright © 2021 by Stanlei Bellan
All rights reserved.

Library of Congress Control Number: 2021931630

ISBN 978-1-954109-00-1 (paperback)
ISBN 978-1-954109-01-8 (ebook)
ISBN 978-1-954109-02-5 (large print)
ISBN 978-1-954109-03-2 (hardcover)
ISBN 978-1-954109-04-9 (audiobook)

First Published in Los Angeles, CA, United States
First Edition March 2021

Cover Design by Marcelo Peró & Natacha Lorente

Edited by Alisa Brooks

Published by Imagilore Publishing

PUBLISHING
www.imagilore.com

To all time dreamers who came before me,
especially the loving Marta and Nelson,
who dreamt of me.

CONTENTS

Another Time _____ 1

Time to Light _____ 7

Time Cleaners _____ 15

Only Time Will Tell _____ 29

Wishful Timing _____ 33

Wild Times _____ 47

Time for Everything _____ 61

Better Luck Next Time _____ 67

Tempus Pompeius _____ 81

Behind the Timestream _____ 103

Timely Story Notes_____ 109

Acknowledgments _____ 117

"A short story is the ultimate close-up magic trick – a couple of thousand words to take you around the universe or break your heart."

—Neil Gaiman

Another Time

ANOTHER MINUTE, another jump.

It's been three minutes and Ollie still hasn't woken up. Granted, he is extremely aware of his surroundings, and doesn't feel like he's dreaming at all, but it would be great if this was a nightmare.

From what he can gather, from his underinformed point of view, he is inside a clock. Not a clock tower, or a cuckoo clock; not even one of those large, standing clocks you see in old haunted houses in horror movies. He is inside what appears to be a plain, round, white wall clock, with big black numbers, made of cheap plastic and cheaper glass. Ollie thought of them as office clocks for people with no imagination.

Another minute, another jump.

This clock is not on a wall but sitting face up on what Ollie assumes is a table. Which is why he has to jump every damn minute. The second hand is so long that it leaves no space whatsoever between its point and the wall of the clock; therefore, every sixty seconds, he has to jump so the hand doesn't hit him.

It is true that instead of jumping he could just keep walking, following the second hand around. But then, every minute, he would have to jump twice: Once every time he crossed paths with the minute hand and again with the hour hand. Not to mention the energy he'd burn walking.

Another minute, another jump.

Much better to stand still, pondering his situation, and jumping once per revolution of the second hand. But maybe it is time to end the pondering – and start the pounding.

Ollie jumps and punches the clock's glass face, which is just a few feet above his head. He is finally putting his class ring, a heavy and pointless metal monstrosity from his obscure university, to use. The transparent dome doesn't break, as he foolishly expected, but he can see a small crack where he hit it. He has something to work with.

Another minute, another jump, another punch.

The glass shatters, sprinkling pain over him. If this is a dream, it is the most uncomfortable one he's had in his life – also the most colorful, as bright red blood blooms from his cut arms. Colorful, but not serious.

And with the pain comes the gain. He is free. Free from the clock, that is; not from his quandary. For some irrational reason, he expected that breaking the glass would end this hallucination. It has not.

As a matter of fact, not much has really changed. He is still inside the laid-down clock, the hands are still moving, and the second hand is approaching.

Another minute, another jump.

One step at a time, he thinks, half smiling at his unintended pun. He has to get out of the clock. The outer wall is an infuriating height: low enough that he can reach it with his fingertips, but too tall to get a grip on. And since he is athletically challenged, there is no way he can lift himself up with just a few fingers.

His only hope is to climb the hands, but that leads to some challenges. Ollie hasn't broken the whole dome; he's only managed to open a small hole in the glass, just past two o'clock. The hands are flexible, and he is pretty sure the only way they can hold his weight is if they are all aligned on top of each other. Right now it's seven thirty-one.

Another minute, another jump, another grunt.

Time is heavy. Ollie decides he cannot wait almost nine hours until the hands align themselves. He is going to take time into his own hands. So he pushes. First the minute hand, clockwise from the thirty-one mark all the way around. He leaves it between the eleven and twelve minute mark.

If the minute hand was hard, the hour hand is almost impossible. There is not as nearly as much leverage as he had with the minute hand, as in this particular clock the hour hand is very short. But after much effort, he gets them aligned.

Another minute, a final jump.

Instead of jumping over the second hand, he jumps onto it, just as it ticks over the minute hand, which in turn sits above the hour hand. Each one bends on top of the other, under Ollie's weight, and then springs back up, like a trampoline, propelling him through the hole in the glass and out of the clock.

He lands on top of the outside wall of the clock and

despairs.

The Clockmaker is watching him. Closely.

"Well done, well done," the thunderous voice echoes around the infinite wooden walls lined with clocks of every size, shape, taste, color, and sound that have ever been built, and some that have yet to be imagined.

The gigantic fingers of the Clockmaker pinch Ollie's shirt and lift him up for a closer inspection.

The eyes of the Clockmaker shine like two moons, protected behind peculiar brass spectacles, thick as binoculars and layered with adjustable loupes and lenses that stick out at all angles.

The Clockmaker, still holding Ollie, navigates through the myriad clocks scattered over the floor, tables, chairs, and shelves, stopping over a very complex piece of clockwork. He holds Ollie dangling, the clock just below his feet.

It is a horizontal clock, mimicking a Victorian city. Like any respectable miniature model (miniature at the scale of the Clockmaker), it is extremely detailed, with its own clock tower, lifting bridges, mechanical birds, and smoking chimneys atop metal houses.

The time is kept by twelve allegories, constructed out of an intricate mix of gears and springs, representing the twelve signs of the zodiac. They are spaced equidistantly over a train track, continuously moving clockwise around the circular city.

The Clockmaker opens a small section of the crystalline quartz dome that covers the city and gently lowers Ollie inside.

Ollie looks up as The Clockmaker closes the dome again and moves away out of view. He is sighing as he scans the city, which is not quite at his own scale, when the clockwork allegory representing Libra comes to life and strikes the bell three times.

Another time. Another escape.

Time to Light

GRIDA CLIMBED the steep, bare stone steps of the lighthouse, around and around. It was a very tall lighthouse. Sunset was just a couple of hours from bending down the infinite horizon. And the light had to be lit.

Slightly out of breath, Grida arrived at the Watch Room. Gathering a small toolbox, some rags, and a flask containing her father's cleaning concoction, she started the last leg of her vertical trip and climbed into the Lantern Room.

Maintenance was severely past due on the whole lantern. Ever since her father's stroke, she'd barely had the time to take care of him, her younger brothers, and their house every day – and to keep the light on every night.

She started on the Fresnel lens, carefully removing the carbon deposits using her father's recipe and a clean rag. She oiled the manual clockwork pump, trimmed the wick, and refueled the tank with enough vegetable oil to last a couple of days. She stood back, satisfied, a nagging pang of anxiety finally drifting away. It was the first time she'd cleaned the lighthouse's lantern by herself.

At eighteen, Grida was proud of taking on her father's responsibilities, but she was also filled with longing. As she looked out of the Lantern Room into the vastness of the ocean, she still wasn't sure what she longed for.

Tinderbox in hand (her father was still suspicious of those so-called Lucifer Matches – 'Nothing with that name could be a good thing!'), she turned to light the wick.

"Stop! Don't light that lantern!" A middle-aged woman's head popped up from the trapdoor to the Watch Room.

Grida's heart skipped a few beats. If the tinderbox hadn't bounced against her foot, she might not have realized she'd dropped it.

"Who are you? What are you doing here?"

"My name is Carol Duncam, and I represent the government. I was sent here to tell you not to light the lantern," the woman explained, climbing up into the Lantern Room and facing Grida.

Grida stared at her for a long, silent moment. She wore an impeccably stylish gray dress, complemented by a pair of sapphire earrings and a matching blue necklace. She wasn't out of breath from her climb, and not a hair was out of place; she radiated calm, controlled authority. For that moment Grida hesitated, almost under the spell of her command. Almost. The next moment she burst out, "That is nonsense! Why would the government ask for such a thing?" She bent to retrieve the tinderbox. "And how do I know you are from the government? You have never come here before." She opened the tinderbox with more force than was strictly necessary. "The lighthouse keeps the boats safe. That is what is important, and it is already getting late."

The woman's expression became at once fierce and fearful. Her voice was authoritative. "I am telling you not to light that lantern. If you do, your life will never be the same."

Grida took a breath and hoped she sounded confident. "Look, ma'am, we can go down to the house and you can say whatever you want to my pop. But there is no chance in heaven that I am not going to light this lantern. It has never been dark after sunset since the day I was born, and tonight will not be the first night."

Grida struck the flint against the steel bar with all the fear and determination she felt rushing through her. A spark flew and touched the wick. The lantern had been lit.

As light and heat flooded the small, windowed room, quickly making it uncomfortable, both women climbed down to the Watch Room. Grida turned to face the stranger, bracing herself for whatever consequences were coming.

"Congratulations, Grida," said Carol, clapping her hands. She was looking at the young lightkeeper's daughter with a mischievous grin. "You fulfilled your duty in spite of a stranger's menace. As I was sure you would."

Grida, who had been mentally practicing one or two things to say to this rude woman, was speechless. A rare thing indeed.

"And you were right, I am not from the government. At least, not the government you are thinking of. But there was one thing I didn't lie about: your life will never be the same."

It was a crisp, cloudy spring morning. The sun had not yet

properly showed its face, stubbornly refusing to dissipate the light, spitting rain. From their point of view at the top of a small hill, Grida and Carol could see the whole of the tiny village right down to the lighthouse at the edge of the cliff.

"What matter of sorcery is this?" Grida breathed, gripping Carol's arm with both hands. "It was night. We were … we were up in the lighthouse! How are we out here? How is it morning?"

To Grida's credit, the questions tumbling from her mouth were asked more out of curiosity than fear. Although, she would later concede, her hands were shaking a wee bit.

"No sorcery. Science. Look." Carol pointed below them, to a commotion unfolding.

At this early hour, the tiny village was swarming with what looked like every single resident. Everyone was going into and out of the only barn in the area.

Blankets and hot soup were being distributed to wet men in uniforms and wet men in street clothes … and a few in coats hastily thrown over sleepwear.

Carol directed Grida's attention once again, this time to the sea. A fresh shipwreck was jutting off of the nearby rocks. The ship's hull, broken in its midsection, looked like a half-eaten porcupine corpse.

Grida stared, agape. She knew that ship. Its features were etched in her mind forever. She also knew the girl who was now rowing that small boat, bringing a couple more rescued sailors from the shipwreck into the safety of the pier. Of course she knew. How could she forget the first time she saved a man's life?

"Yes," said Carol softly. "The year is eighteen-thirty-one,

and that is the Fortshire." She pointed to the recently wrecked ship, and then brought her finger down to the pier level. "And that barely adolescent girl, rowing against all the forces of nature and mankind, is the reason I am here."

"Is this a dream?" It was the only thing she could think of to ask.

"Pay attention now. You are just finishing tying that rowboat to the pier, and the village elder is coming to reprimand you. Do you remember what you said to him?" Carol asked, ignoring Grida's question.

"A donkey …" Grida half murmured, half whispered.

"Yes. Donkey indeed." Carol's expression was contained, but it failed to hide the spark in her eyes "Here, take my hand again," she offered, reaching for one of Grida's and with her other hand pulling out a strange rectangular pocket watch. She flipped the gem-inlaid cover open, exposing the machinery of the device. It was like no watch Grida had ever seen: hundreds of tiny cogs and springs moved at different speeds and in different directions. She turned a knob a few times, pressed a tiny lever on the side, and closed the lid with a loud click.

The storm was raging furiously and sheets of freezing water poured onto the sturdy boat. The lighthouse's lantern and the near-constant lightning in the clouds were the only glimmers piercing the nocturnal darkness; the former brought hope, the latter despair.

Carol and Grida were now standing on the edge of the pier, the chill rain washing away any lingering doubt that Grida might be dreaming. Suddenly, a rope snapped up close to their feet, pulled taut by a rowboat already several yards away in the turbulent waters.

In the boat, Grida could see a younger version of herself struggling with the oars, as the young lightkeeper's daughter realized she hadn't completely freed the rowboat from the pier. In the distance, the Fortshire, in flames, was already stranded on the rocks.

"Help!" The younger Grida's shout barely reached the older Grida's ears. She remembered, of course. She had never found out who had untied her rowboat that night. Nobody in the village would take credit. She always assumed it had been an angel.

Grida quickly crouched and released the rope, freeing her daredevil younger self to go and save the sailors. She could not hear over the tempest, but she knew she had shouted her thanks.

Carol put her hand on Grida's shoulder, and once again they vanished.

"It is not much different from the machinery of your lighthouse. It is just … much more complex. It is still only a machine, though. A tool." Carol closed Grida's fingers over the clockwork box resting in her palm.

"A tool that can travel through time," Grida repeated, trying to convince herself.

Carol was surprised by how quickly Grida had come to terms with everything. It was a testament to how right Carol had been to have pushed for her recruitment.

"And you want me to have one of these?" Grida asked.

"More than that. I want you to become an agent of good through time." Carol finally explained. "You see, history is filled with small moments that can tip humankind to a darker, bleaker path. I work for an organization that has vowed to prevent that. In order to do so, we need people like yourself, who are willing to risk their own lives to save others."

"But why me? Why now?"

"Because this is not an effortless task. Those who travel through time face a heavy physical and mental burden. We need agents who are not only dutiful, but, most importantly, people who are strongly grounded." Carol waved her hand to take in the lighthouse, shining its light under the clear starry sky.

Looking up at the beacon brought Grida back to reality. "I have responsibilities with my pop and my brothers. And the lighthouse. I could never leave them," she replied, surprised by the sadness she felt.

"I am not asking you to leave them," Carol said, smiling a slow, wild smile. "I wouldn't want you to." She tapped the device in Grida's hand. "With this, you can go on countless adventures, help history maintain its true north – and always be back in time to light the lantern."

Grida's favorite spot in the whole world was still in the Lantern Room, looking deep into the endless sea. But unlike when she was a young woman, she no longer looked out with longing.

She had been the officially appointed lightkeeper for many decades now, after her father passed away. Her brothers were all fine men, each with their own lives and families. And the lighthouse never failed to light the way, not for a single moment, each night when darkness fell.

Grida was getting old now. It was time to find herself a

replacement, and she had a good idea of where to start looking.

Without a glance at the gem-inlaid device, she turned a knob a few times and pressed the tiny lever on its side. But just before she closed the lid with a loud click, she once again lit the lantern.

> *"None – but a donkey, would consider it*
> *'un-feminine' to save lives."*
>
> —Ida Lewis, the young lightkeeper's daughter, responding to criticism that it was un-ladylike for women to row boats.

Time Cleaners

THE BATTERED ELECTRONIC PANEL flashed again, shifting the previous orders down. A short buzz marked the display of the next assignment number, followed by a crackle over the waiting room speakers: "Number thirty-one, number thirty-one, present your license at window forty-two."

"Come on, Mary, that's us." John kicked at his partner, who was soundly snoring. After all these years, he still couldn't understand how she could sleep in the waiting room. It was always packed with people, smelled of freshly splattered rotten cabbage, and the damn panel's buzzing was more maddening than a slow drip of water hammering softly but relentlessly on your brain.

"When are we going?" Mary half-yawned, half-asked as she brushed the sleep out of her eyes.

"How would I know? I still can't find my license,

remember? Window forty-two." John pointed up at the panel.

"Oh, yeah, yeah. Okay, I'm going." Mary stood up as the panel blinked and beeped their number.

"Number thirty-one, number thirty-one, present your license at window forty-two." The monotonous clerk's voice came over the speakers again, this time with an edge of coming doom to be rained upon whoever was making her day even slower.

"Geez, I'm coming," Mary shouted as she approached window forty-two. "I'm here, happy?"

The distinctly unhappy clerk didn't bother responding. She checked Mary's license and handed over her assignment slip without uttering a single syllable.

"The verdict?" John asked as Mary returned. She opened the slip of paper and showed it to him. "Hey, that's a new one!"

They moved out of the waiting room and into a large hallway lined on both walls with maintenance lockers which had maybe seen better days, but if so, they'd been a century ago. They checked the slip of paper again and soon found the right locker.

Leaving their stuff on the top shelf, they quickly removed their uniforms and slowly dressed in the old garments inside the locker. From other shelves they grabbed two large buckets, already filled with a milky mixture, and two very old-fashioned mops. John shouldered a large tote filled with rags, soap bars, and various cleaning liquids.

"Hey, did you check the weather?" John asked, trying to keep up with Mary, who was striding down a long corridor filled with doors sporting electronic keypad locks. Mary didn't hear him – or at least she acted as if she hadn't – and only stopped when they arrived at their designated door.

"Ready?" It was a rhetorical question asked out of habit while she punched the codes from the assignment slip into the keypad.

With a long beep and a loud click, the door unlocked. Mary opened it, since John was carrying the buckets, and a draft of chill air blew past them.

"You didn't check the weather, did you?" he complained, crossing the door's frame.

Mary sighed and rolled her eyes as she followed, closing the door behind them.

"What a mess!" John rested the buckets on the carpeted floor as he absorbed the scene around him.

"Well, now we know why they gave us the large buckets," Mary said, coming in behind him. Neither of them paid any attention as the outline of the door, which had appeared in the middle of the room, gradually vanished into thin air.

John and Mary were properly unionized employees of TTC[2] Inc., the famous Time Travel Corps Squared Incorporated. Which, since the unexpected demise of TTC[1] Inc., was the sole company in control of time travel technology.

TTC[2] had it all: time tourism, time scavenging, time safari, time exploration, time trading, and many other divisions among several – all lucrative – business endeavors. And to keep all of that working without messing with history (well … too much, that is), they also had their most coveted division: the Time Agents.

The Time Agents were highly trained personnel,

handpicked from the best universities, companies, and military organizations across the globe. They freely traveled up and down the timestream, avoiding paradoxes, arresting time hooligans, and erasing hardcore time extremists. They were the only ones licensed to erase.

John was profoundly proud of the Time Agents. He just wasn't one of them. He and Mary were members of the absolutely not coveted Time Cleaners division. They were the ones who made sure that any time mess (anachronistic or time shifted DNA materials) left behind from a Time Agent mission was properly mopped up.

And that is how they ended up in room 429 of The Grand Brighton Hotel, in the United Kingdom, in the Autumn of 1984. The room looked as if Matisse, in his later years, had painted the killing grounds of a pig slaughterhouse. The dull yellows of the patterned wallpaper, the highly intricate and exquisitely cut furniture, and the insanely tasteless chandeliers were all smeared with blood, sweat, and other bodily fluids (and parts).

"What the hell happened here?" Mary asked, disheartened at the thought of cleaning the entire room. This was a suite with several rooms, a king bed draped with tapestries, and more furniture than she could catalog in a glance.

"As always, not a single mention on our assignment slip. They are just adamant that we can't make any loud noise or leave this room. Apparently, no one will come in here until tomorrow. A time door will open again at 2:50 a.m." John pressed a hidden button on his otherwise chronologically correct watch. "Local time is 12:01 a.m."

"This must have been a tremendous fight, between at least five or six people," Mary commented, putting on a rubber glove and wetting one rag in the special milky substance from the buckets. It smelled faintly of pine and would completely erase any anachronistic DNA from the scene. "Any idea why this moment in time is important?"

"No idea," John said, "but I think I can figure it out." He grinned, and took a small pad out of his pocket, "Let's see what happened here in Brighton on October 12th, 1984."

"What are you doing with a history pad again?" Mary chastised him, forcefully scrubbing a large desk. "If management catches you with it, I'm not supporting you this time."

"How am I supposed to become a Time Agent if they don't allow me to learn history?"

Mary's voice was bitter as she said, "They're never going to let us be Time Agents. They're never even going to look at our applications, let alone give us an interview. We're not Time Agent material." She scrubbed the desk harder.

But John was unmoved by her pessimism. (Possibly because this was a conversation they had no fewer than three times a week.) "Ah! Of course. This was the site of the assassination attempt against Margaret Thatcher and the whole UK cabinet," John reported, using his mop as a makeshift crutch – without using it to clean an inch of the room. "It's a well-known target for time extremists, as they believe a disruption at this moment would generate a chain of events that could avoid the Terrorist Wars."

"Why do they keep trying to change history? The Time Agents never fail, because they can just keep trying and trying until they succeed. And beyond that there's the PIP."

"Well, not all time travelers actually believe in laws, or history, or science, for that matter. And let's be realistic, if you had never seen the aftereffects of the Paradoxical Implosion Principle yourself, would you believe in it?" John asked as he walked around the room, still not cleaning anything.

"We should take some pictures of this room and put them on the dark timeweb, so at least some of these extremists would think twice. Might make our life easier." Mary was mopping the floor at full steam. "I bet that big splash over there is from someone trying to set off a bomb or something. They got imploded."

The PIP was the main source of sorrow for the Time Cleaners. Basically, the past was somewhat malleable and could be changed in small ways, but if anybody attempted to make a big change, the Paradoxical Implosion Principle, or PIP, would come into play and literally implode whoever was trying to damage the timestream. Nobody really knew why or how it worked. Hence the skeptics and conspiracy theorists saying it was all an invention of TTC[2].

Finally, Mary noticed that John had not moved a muscle to help her. She slapped him on the back of the head and added, "And if you don't start cleaning, right now, you will be the next thing to implode in this room."

John started cleaning. He decided to tackle a big puddle of blood under a massive mahogany table. It was as good a place as any to start ... especially because it would block Mary from seeing him dabbling with his history pad.

Not surprisingly, his cleaning performance was inversely proportional to how engaging a particular story about Margaret Thatcher became. When Mary slapped the table above him, he jumped, hit his head on the underside of the table, and fell, butt first, into the puddle of blood.

"Dammit, Mary! I was cleaning, I was cleaning!" he

complained under Mary's hearty laughter. "I was just taking a brea–" he stopped mid-sentence, the hand he'd pushed into the blood for leverage frozen stiffly. "Oh, no. I think I just pressed on a Time Mine."

"Are you kidding? That's perfect!" Mary said, cheerfully dropping her mop to shuffle in her pocket for her license. "We can use the extra time to check out their entertainment set. Here's my license, when you're done with yours."

"What license, you dimwit?" John tried to maintain his usual joking tone, but he was pale and his voice was thin. "I don't have mine. I lost it, remember?"

Everything drained out of Mary's face – cheer, breath, color. She stood silent, her trembling hand raised to her mouth, too stunned to speak.

The Time Mine was a particularly efficient tool of mass erasure. When triggered, it released a cloud of nanobots that consumed any and all biological matter with a chronologically displaced signature. In other words, it erased time travelers.

To prevent these mines from being used against employees, the company had designed them with a simple bypass: agents and cleaners could tap their license on the mine and the nanobots would completely ignore their DNA. This system worked so well that the Time Cleaners division regularly sent requests to TTC^2 management asking to use Time Mines in their day-to-day cleaning work, as they would considerably reduce their time-to-clean KPIs. These requests were invariably denied; aside from the fact that the Time Agents would never allow it, cleaning personnel were far cheaper than Time Mines.

John spoke first. "Snap out of it, Mary. We need to figure this out. Quickly."

"There's nothing to figure out, John," Mary said, lowering her hand and swallowing hard. "You just need to stay calm. Don't move until our time door pops back open. Then I'll go back to HQ and bring someone here to disarm it."

"That's not for another three hours!" John shouted.

"Well," she said, trying to smile, "good thing you're sitting down, right?"

———————— ⧗ ————————

Mary had carefully cleaned the area around John, so he could be more comfortable and she could sit down beside him. She also cleaned enough blood off the Time Mine to allow her to tap her own license on it. With a harmless beep, her DNA was registered.

"At least if it goes off, you won't be erased." John half smiled at her.

"Don't even say that. Everything will work out just fine," Mary replied, knocking three times on the wooden table above their heads. "What I want to know is how our 'perfect' Time Agents left this thing behind. Oh, I am going to make sure everyone knows about this. We should sue the company into the ground for this."

"Yeah, you're right." John looked at a surprised Mary and went on. "It doesn't make sense. I mean, if the Time Agents slipped up, we'll definitely sue. But they wouldn't have. We've got to be missing something. Here, take the history pad and check out what happened today."

Mary took the pad and read out loud.

"At approximately 2:54 a.m., a bomb, set by IRA agents,

will detonate in room 629. The explosion will cause part of the chimney stack, several tons of brick, to collapse through all the lower floors, destroying a good part of the hotel, and killing several people from the UK government. The Prime Minister and her husband will only suffer minor scratches, because the debris will miss their bedroom, destroying their bathroom instead." She paused and then turned to John. "Which room are we in again?"

"429. We're right below the explosion! That's why our return door is at 2:50; after that, there will be no room 429. Go on," John told her, excited enough by history to momentarily forget about the precarious present.

"The bomber did not use enough TNT, and the explosion failed to bring down the whole hotel, which was their goal. There were nine instant casualties and dozens of injured people."

"That's what must have happened here," John said. "Time extremists must have tried to augment the explosion and were stopped by the Time Agents. What doesn't make sense is why WE are here. If this entire room will be destroyed in the bombing, why did management send us here to clean it? It will make absolutely no difference whose blood is whose under all that debris."

Almost three hours had passed quickly once they got used to the fact that a sneeze could erase John from existence. They'd sat, talking comfortably, meandering over well-worn subjects, bickering and joking.

"Remember our date?" Mary asked, nudging John..

Now his heart beat faster. "Which one?" He knew which one.

"Our first month working together. That little escapade after the job in Brazil? We were so awkward." Mary laughed self-consciously, while John fought with himself. Should he keep ignoring it, as he had all these years? Aw, what the hell – what did he have to lose?

"How could I forget it, Mary?" His voice was quiet, and he felt heat creeping up his neck in spite of himself. "I think about it every day."

Mary was shocked. "But … you shook my hand! You said we should be friends. You weren't interested …"

"I was interested." He shrugged away his insecurity, the crushing fear. "I didn't think you were and I … I didn't want to mess up what we had."

"You idiot." But Mary was smiling wide, things finally clicking into place.

"I still have it, you know?" John pulled a yin-yang amulet, made of citrine and silver, out of an inner pocket. They'd found it in the Brazilian cleaning scene, and Mary had said that it looked like sunlight trapped in night, like fireflies in a jar. Light in the darkness. John had stood, dazed by her smile, until she turned back to work, and then he'd promptly stolen the necklace. It was the only time he'd ever taken something from work; he could easily have been fired and charged if it had been discovered. He'd never regretted it for a moment.

"You kept it?" She was shaking her head gently, still disbelieving.

John looked at her, serious. "You're the best part of my day."

She chuckled softly. "You too. Idiot."

At the scheduled time, faithful as the moon, the outline of the time door materialized out of nowhere in the middle of the room. Mary tapped John on the leg and got ready to stand up, but John grabbed her hand, holding her back.

Through the time door, two men quickly entered and scanned the room. They were wearing standard Time Cleaner's uniforms, carrying large backpacks, and holding small hand disphasors.

"They're here," the tallest one said, pointing his disphasor at John and Mary under the table. "Don't move," he added, addressing them.

The short one removed his backpack and offered it to the taller one. "You're better with the bombs. I got them," He finished, taking the taller one's place threatening John and Mary.

He talked nervously as the taller one tied both backpacks together. "It will all be over soon. We just need to prevent the war, you know? This will erase the war. This will change everything. This will show TTC[2] they don't control history."

"Easy man, easy," John said soothingly, his eyes on the disphasor. "We're just cleaners."

"This will prove that we ARE right, that history can be changed. Changed for the better, you know?" The short one was now sweating profusely, his hand slightly trembling. "I'm sorry, but your sacrifice will show them we're right."

"What sacrifice? What are you talking about?" Mary edged closer to John and held his free hand tight.

"We need to show that we can change history. We need history to find you here. It's not personal, you know."

John understood. They wanted John and Mary's bodies to be found in the bombing's aftermath. Future bodies in the past. Mary started crying silently. She understood too.

The taller one finished setting up the backpacks, which John assumed were filled with some kind of explosives, and told the shorter one it was time to go. If they crossed back into the TTC² time hall and closed the door, management would just think John and Mary were returning a bit late from their assignment. No alarms would be raised, no one would come looking for them. They were going to be stuck in the past. They were going to die in the past.

The shorter one walked backward toward the door, still keeping them in his disphasor's aim. "It's not personal."

"Well, this is VERY personal." John turned to Mary and kissed her. Passionately. Deeply. And lifted his hand from the Time Mine.

Mary opened her eyes. Room 429 was clean. The blood and body parts from the fight were gone. The terrorists were also gone, their clothes in pathetically small piles on the floor. John was gone too.

She looked at her watch: 2:53 a.m. She only had one minute before the whole building came crashing down on her head. As she crawled out from under the table, she felt something cold and hard under her hand. It was the amulet.

Mary, safely back in the TTC² time hall, pressed the keypad to lock the time portal. As the lock clicked, she could hear the fading rumble of the explosion on the other side of time.

She looked down at the two backpacks she had dragged to this side. John might be gone forever; but he had done something he'd always dreamed of and she'd never really believed could be done – he had saved the timestream, and he'd proved that even a cleaner could be Time Agent material. Mary would never forget that. Actually, she would make damn sure nobody forgot.

Mary was fidgeting with the citrine amulet when she heard the beep coming from the electronic panel. The clerk was already calling her number, so she went to the window to get her new assignment. The clerk asked for her license, and she showed it to him.

It read Mary P. Sherman, Time Agent.

Only Time Will Tell

"SORRY, YOUR HONOR. I was unwillingly delayed by some matter."

"You are here now, that is all that matters. Will you state your name for the record, please?" Lord Chance requested.

"Wouldn't you agree that more relevant than telling my name would be stating what I have to tell?"

"No telling what that could be if you are not known to the court and, therefore, recognized as the one who can tell," Lord Chance replied.

"I must insist on what will become self-evident: If I indeed manage to tell, such telling will end with my own indisputable recognition."

Lord Chance pondered for a moment. The reasoning was sound, if marginally unorthodox. He was not sure how worthwhile it would be to further postpone the procedure just so the record could be straight. Nevertheless, it was definitely worth raising the stakes.

"Very well, I will concede your motion. The burden of recognition will be upon your telling. If you succeed, your status will be elevated; you will be one of us. If you fail, however, your own identity will be in peril. The peril of non-existence," Lord Chance adjudicated.

The severity of the ruling took all by surprise. Lord EM rubbed his hands with a spark of excitement; the Nuclear Sisters, Lady Strong and Lady Weak, were both charged with contradictory expectations; and finally, Lord Gravity kept to himself, his face grave.

A simple hearing had just become an existential trial. The fleeting witness, who was now the main defendant, started without further ado.

"How can one delineate that which, despite being constantly measured, tricked religion, philosophy, and science into an endless measure of circularity?

"I resent and repeal," the swift defendant continued, "the simplistic definition that I shall be the indefinite continued progress of existence and events that occur in an apparently irreversible succession from the past, through the present, into the future.

"Wherefore, regardless of whatever I may be, I will now tell what needs to be told." The immemorial defendant exhaled, drawing nigh to the conclusion of his telling.

"The absolute continuum, whose own obsidian fabric I am woven into forevermore, cries out for a meaning beyond the singularity of the forward motion. Life does not flow invariably downstream but is actually the alluring amalgamation of all that was, of all that is, and of all that will be. Thence, may it be known that henceforth whoever dreams a new dream, shall not fear previous nightmares, because the past itself shall no longer be immutable, but changeable. Just a light travel away."

The pantheon of Lords and Ladies, entranced by the telling, were snapped back to reality by the sudden dull crash of Lord Chance's gavel, and his unwavering verdict: "It is told."

> *"Only time (whatever that may be) will tell."*
> —Stephen Hawking, *A Brief History of Time*

Wishful Timing

"WELL MET, MASTER. What three trips do you desire?"

"I beg your pardon?"

"I shall grant you three trips."

"Don't you mean three wishes?"

"No, no, no. You must be confusing me with the other kind of djinn. I don't grant wishes; I grant trips."

I will be severely disappointed. And that in itself tells a lot about expectations. I did not go for my morning walk on the beach expecting anything, much less a sharp pain as I stubbed my big toe against something in the sand. But then, after thoroughly cursing the object, I expected to dig up a rock or trash left over from a late-night party. To my surprise, I found a half-buried, ancient, gold oil lamp.

Again, expectations came into play. What do you do

when crossing paths with an ancient lamp? It doesn't matter where you encounter one – a shop, a friend's house, or even a museum if you can get away with it – you rub it. You don't really expect anything to happen, but it's just what you do.

To my continued surprise, my expectations were once again confounded as a purplish, sparkling fog poured out of the antique's tip. Smoke that eventually took the shape of an honest-to-god, gigantic, Arabian-Nights-dressed genie. At this point, I of course expected my three wishes. But that is not what will happen.

"Wishes are overrated," the genie will say, slightly irritated. "Lots of room for confusion if you don't word the wish very carefully. Trips are much better," The genie will add, sensing the dismay of his new master. "You can choose three places and I will instantly transport you there. And, by 'place' I mean anywhere and anytime in the whole expanse and history of the universe."

"Do you mean time travel?"

"Yes!" The genie will reply, excited. "Time AND space travel. Pick a specific location and a specific time, and off you go. Just remember to bring the lamp with you – that is very important, of course."

I will feel excitement creeping back into my bones. But I will not yet be ready to jump on board the whole trip thing.

"First of all, and just for the record, if I did have wishes, I could ask you to use them to send me traveling through time, so I still think wishes are better. But the actual point is: how can I be sure you can deliver on your promise?"

"Oh, a non-believer? No problem, that's why the Djinn's Guild has the long-established tradition of the petite wish." My eyes will brighten for a split second, leading the genie to hastily explain himself. "Wish, of course, in the generic sense. I still only grant trips. But besides your three, I can grant a very short test trip."

I will think I am really going to need to work on my expectations if I am going to emotionally survive all of this.

"Okay. Let's do it then." I will take my cellphone from my back pocket and, using my shoes and some sand, will improvise a camera tripod of sorts and start recording. "Send me three minutes into the future."

"Actually," the genie will reply, slightly embarrassed, "I can't really work with relative time instructions. I need a precise location and a precise time. You see, was it three minutes from the exact instant you stopped speaking, or from the moment I finish my incantation? And if I need to ask any follow-up questions, which happens more than you would think, was it three minutes since then or now?"

I'm a very rational person, so somehow this will make sense. I will go back to my phone, take note of what time it is, add five minutes in my mind, just to be sure of any follow-up questions, and try again.

"Genie of the lamp, transport me to this exact spot at exactly six forty-two a.m. Pacific Standard Time, today, the thirty-first day of August of the two thousand and twentieth year of the Common Era of the Gregorian calendar." I will be very proud of my wording.

The genie will raise both his arms, moving them in grand arcs above his head. He will straighten his posture as the speed of his movements increase, multicolored sparks forming all around him, his face contorting as he clasps his hands together with a thunderous sound, leaving both his index fingers pointing to the heavens. He will start to point them in my direction as he reaches the climax of the magic. I will half turn my head and close my eyes. And then, nothing.

"Sorry." The genie will open his hands, breaking the spell. "May I just clarify a tiny little detail?"

"What?" I will shout, exasperated.

"When you said 'exact same spot,' did you mean this exact same spot on this planet, or this exact same spot in the universe?"

I will blanch with horror. My knuckles will turn white around the cold lamp as I realize my command was not as brilliant as I had thought. Not only does the Earth rotate on its own axis as it orbits the Sun, the Sun itself orbits the center of the Milky Way, which in turn orbits other galaxies – all of that at thousands of miles per second. If the genie followed my instruction to the letter, I would most likely be floating in the vacuum of space or, if I had been really lucky, crushed inside some planet or star that happened to be in this exact same spot, relative to the universe, a little less than five minutes from then.

"I meant," I will barely whisper, raspy words coming from a dry throat, "on this planet."

"Done." The genie will clasp his hands and point his index fingers at me. The previously unreleased magical energy will shoot forward, engulfing me in blinding light.

"It worked!" I will pace left and right as I play the video on my phone repeatedly.

"And that's why we have the small freebie. Very well, master. What is your first trip?"

"What? Are you crazy? I don't know yet! This just got serious. I only have three destinations, and I need to think about where and when I want to go."

I had played several what-if games in my life, like what would I do if I won the lottery, or which famous actor I would like to spend the night with, or where would I go on my honeymoon, if I ever find the right person. But I'd never considered what to do if I had a time machine, even one powered by a second-rate genie.

As I think about it, I will realize that, in fact, I have only two trips. I love my life and am a very happy young woman, with a promising scientific career. I have friends and family that I am not willing to lose, so wherever this adventure takes me, I will need to use one of the trips to come back. Yes, I will decide, the third trip would be to send me back to where I started.

My sense of accomplishment for making my first, or actually last, trip decision, will quickly be overcome by the realization that so far I have only procrastinated my other decisions. The truth is that I will still have no idea where I should go.

"Master?" The genie will ask, with that face waiters make when you are reading the menu for half an hour and still haven't made up your mind. "The first trip?"

"Look, this might take some time. Don't you want to take a walk or something? Aren't you tired of being inside the lamp?"

"Actually, it is quite comfortable inside. After a strike lasting a couple millennia, the guild had to improve our accommodations. We are still fighting for equal benefits, though. But I digress, my worry is about your trips. Every time you rub the lamp, you are required to make at least one formal request before the first sunset of your current location – if such location is a celestial body with sunsets, that is. The Djinn's Guild is rather strict about that, I am afraid."

Expectation management is clearly not in the guild's training manual.

"Genie, what other rules do I need to know?"

"Let me see," The genie will pause, counting fingers on one hand, "I can only transport you and whatever you are able to carry with you. Every trip is instantaneous, final, and nonreturnable. If another person rubs the lamp and requests a trip before you make your third trip, you lose any unused trips. And finally, if I witness you about to create any kind of time paradox, you will be completely erased from history. That's it! Simple, right? Now, where are we going?"

I will freeze again. This is getting more and more serious by the minute. For just an instant I will think about abandoning the whole thing, driving to a very tall cliff, and throwing the lamp and the genie far, far away. But I will not let this opportunity pass me by. I'll decide that all I need is a very detailed plan; after I figure out where I want to go.

"Okay. I still have almost half a day to decide," I'll say. When I notice the genie looking impatient, I will add, "And I plan to use every single minute of it. So, either go back to your lamp or come along, but give me some breathing room."

The genie will sigh, but eventually reply with proper respect. "Yes. Master." The genie will snap his fingers and decrease in size as his clothes, hair, and facial features become that of a stereotypical Californian surfer dude, if a look that typical even exists. He will snap his fingers again and a nicely crafted sun umbrella will show up in his hand, already open above both of us. "Much better. No need to draw unwanted attention, right?"

"Wait a minute, can you do other kinds of magic besides

granting trips?"

"Sure I can. Just not for you. Well, not unless I get a long-overdue promotion; only djinns of level five or above have permission to do so."

'If you could travel through time, where would you go?'

I will not even have to finish typing before the search engine automatically fills phrases in for me. There will be thousands of pages of comments and opinions.

'I would go back and spend more time and get to know my grandparents better.'

Cute, but too domestic.

'Late 1700s – Beethoven, Mozart, etc.'

Too musical.

'I would return to Dallas Texas on November 22, 1963 and stop the Kennedy assassination.'

Too political.

'Jerusalem 31 C.E., of course. Being a Christian, I would suppose most others would choose the same.'

Too religious.

'I would go to Hawaii in the 60s and surf my brains out and live off the land.'

Too hippie.

'I would go fishing with Hemingway and drink some good Spanish wine.'

Too idyllic.

'I would time travel into the early years of America and try to free slaves and break down color, race, gender, and sexuality barriers.'

Wow.

The internet search will not help me at all. Beyond the expected key historic events and people, I will read lots and lots of emotional stories of people wanting to go back in time to save a loved one, or to stop themselves from making a terrible life choice. But most of these scenarios will not actually take all the consequences of such travels into account. They were not thinking it through because they did not have a way of doing it. I will.

At least having the genie-turned-surfer with me will have a few extra benefits. I will be able to further investigate the nitty-gritty details of time travel.

First, as I have already learned, I will need to give very specific location instructions. According to the genie (paraphrasing), "He is not a time travel agent, nor a Google Maps of history." I can't say, "Send me to Leonardo da Vinci's studio." I would have to say something like, "Send me to the garden of the Piazza San Marco in Firenze, Repubblica Fiorentina." And pick a time when he would be painting there in order to actually find the man. Also of note, I would have to find the correct country, which in this case would not be Italy, because Italy hadn't been founded yet. So, it would be tricky.

But that is not all. Clothing and language are not part of the package (which is such a common complaint, by previous lamp masters, that according to the genie, the guild is seriously considering including it, probably in a century or so).

I only speak English, Portuguese, and bits and pieces of French. That alone will almost entirely remove most of the distant past, and plenty of other very interesting places. Unless, of course, I want to play the lost immigrant. But the risks are fairly high of something unpleasant happening; history does not have a track record of being super nice to women through the ages.

None of that will matter. I won't allow such an opportunity to pass me by without making the most of it. The only way of doing it will be to be honest with myself. I cannot regret my choices.

I will leave the genie experimenting with my Apple TV, go to my bathroom, close the toilet seat lid, and sit on it. I will close my eyes and reach deep, deep inside.

"Genie of the lamp. Transport me to this exact spot, on this planet, at exactly six a.m. Pacific Standard Time, on the thirty-first day of August of the two thousand and fortieth year of the Common Era of the Gregorian calendar," I will order, standing on the sand, roughly where I found the lamp just a few hours before. And to my utter satisfaction, for the first time, there will be no follow-up questions from the genie.

The momentary blindness from the spell's effect will subside in a few moments, and I will see a middle-aged woman, wearing a cap and sunglasses, approaching me.

"Just like I remember. I can't believe I was ever that young." She – me, future me, in my forties – will remove her sunglasses, approach me – her younger self – and unceremoniously hug me tightly.

I will panic, fearful of being erased out of existence, until my older self explains, "It's okay. Hugging does not cause paradoxes. There is no such a thing as the same person occupying the same space. Lots of quantum space between the two of us, even this close."

"Wow, I am glad to see you – I mean me – here. Did it work then? Aren't you excited?" I will ask.

"Yes, it worked. More than you will know for a long

time," the older me will reply, stepping back from the hug. "And, no, I'm not that excited. From my point of view, this has already happened. What I am, though, is deeply grateful for our decision."

"Really?"

"One hundred percent," the older me will confirm. "You should definitely follow our plan."

"Any more advice?"

"The same as always. Keep looking forward."

I will look deep into my own older eyes and see that I'm happy. That will be enough for now. I will also notice a few other details, as I rub the magical lamp: The odd fashion of the T-shirt my forty-year-old self is wearing, the diamond ring on my older left hand, and the three kids in the distance clearly looking at us.

"Genie of the lamp. Transport me to this exact same spot, on this planet, at exactly six a.m. Pacific Standard Time, on the thirty-first day of August of the two thousand one hundred and fortieth year of the Common Era of the Gregorian calendar."

———————— ⧖ ————————

Confusion …

   … cold …

   … desperation …

   … water …

   … drowning.

My eyes will spasm open as I regurgitate gallons of salt water onto a polished wood deck. A nice young man, standing slightly over me, will turn me sideways to help me spit it all out. After some coughing, followed by a warm blanket and an even warmer cup of tea, my mind will clear.

That's when it will hit me.

"The lamp! Where is the lamp? Have you seen a lamp?" I will beg in a raspy voice, realizing for the first time I am sitting, soaked, on the back deck of a very fancy yacht, surrounded by half a dozen people.

"Easy now. Everything's fine." The strong young man who helped me will be totally at ease. "Your lamp is safe and sound. Even half-drowned you wouldn't let it go; I had to literally rip it from your arms so I could get you breathing again."

"Where am I?" I will still be disoriented.

"You are exactly where you asked to be," a very old woman, being pushed close to me in a wheelchair, will tell me in an unsteady voice. "In the exact same spot." The ancient matriarch will smile before continuing, "The problem is that the same exact spot, nowadays, is under water. Talk about greenhouse effect, huh?"

"Wow." My thoughts will catch up with me, as I scold myself mentally for not picking a spot a little farther from the sea line. "Well, clearly I didn't stop climate change."

"No. But you helped a lot ..." the old woman will comfort me, taking my hand in her own frail ones, "... mom."

I have never been on a yacht before, especially not one from the mid 22nd century, and I will definitely enjoy the experience. I will be back in my own dry clothes, after a very long shower in what they called a "surround bathtub," sitting in the boat's living room and facing a coastline I no longer recognized.

"Apparently a lot has changed," I will offer, feeling that

all these strangers looking at me are waiting for me to say something.

"I guess so," my elderly daughter will reply, "but when you live as long as I have, you end up seeing things through different lenses. Despite all the cosmetic changes in the world's evolution, nothing actually changes on a more fundamental level." The old lady will pause for effect before adding, "Guess who taught me that?"

I will smile uncomfortably.

"You know, I was at the beach that day. Exactly one hundred years ago, which obviously reveals more about my age than I'd normally share." The old woman will blink at me, "My mom ... I mean you – or rather, an older you – made a point for all of us, my siblings and I, to be there that day. You wanted so much for us to believe in the future. But even after they saw the lights, the genie, and the disappearing act – it all faded from their minds. Over time they thought of it as a childish daydream, and then they forgot altogether. Not me, though.

"I kept believing in you. Not only believing, but also working hard toward everything you taught me." The old lady will wave her hand, indicating all the people assembled as well as the ridiculously spacious room on the yacht. "Everyone here is your direct descendant. The young man who fished you out of the water is your great-great-grandson."

My daughter will look around the room. "And believe me when I say, not many of those who are here today truly believed you would show up in a flash of light, under the water."

"Unfortunately, I believe we have already pressed our luck a bit too much. Every minute you stay increases your risk." The elderly matriarch will point to the lamp on top of a small table. "It's time to go back. You have been wise in your choices, and I'm sure you will be again. Just remember to look forward."

My great-great-grandson will drop me, via flyboat (which is amazing), on a nearby rock outcropping that had stubbornly remained unsubmerged. I will have millions of questions, including all their names, but I will know better than to ask.

I will summon the genie and give the command for the last trip, arriving back in the past moments after I rubbed the lamp for the first time.

From this vantage point, I can see myself disappearing into the five-minute test trip, which is much more impressive to witness than to experience.

I look at the now-useless lamp in my hand, and without further thought throw it back into the ocean, a long way below the high cliff that will become that small rock outcropping in a little less than a century and a half.

I am satisfied with my decisions. The first trip had been risky, as I might have died before my fortieth birthday (which, thankfully, was not the case). The second, just by meeting my still-living daughter, was immensely rewarding. And since the genie has not erased me from existence, all that I learned is apparently fair game.

And I did learn a lot.

It is not every day that you know, with certainty, that your legacy will endure.

It is also not every day you are given hope that the future is worth fighting for.

And finally, as I had bet on from the beginning, it is also

not every day you are one hundred percent positive which companies will be around for the next twenty years, and again for another century.

After all, not only will my forty-year-old self be wearing a very specific set of clothing and accessories, carefully chosen to display the brands which will be most successful in the next twenty years; but everyone in that yacht is, or will be, wearing the hottest brands that will survive all that time.

My next step will be to find out how to buy stocks, as I've never done it before. And then go redefine the meaning of expected returns.

Wild Times

"THIS IS IT. This is it! I finally figured it out! Are you ready? We will launch in four minutes!" The old, fat professor was almost vibrating with excitement, shouting a running stream of commentary to his not-so-old guinea pig. And by guinea pig I mean, of course, me. Harold Archie Ladgrove III (which reads 'Harold Archie Ladgrove the Third,' just so you know). Not that anyone has called me that for a long time. That's a story for another time. These days, I'm simply Hal.

"Hal, look lively girl! You are about to make history!" Bob was a good man, but a not-great scientist. Nothing about him lived up to the scientist image; even his name sounded wrong. But according to the diplomas on the walls, he had been to Harvard, MIT, and Stanford. What the diplomas don't tell, though, is that he had been expelled from each one of those institutions. Because at each one,

47

though it had eventually been hushed up out of sheer embarrassment, he had been caught relentlessly misappropriating their money, research, and resources to develop a time machine.

"Three minutes to go. Checklist time!" I went through the motions just to make Bob happy. You see, we had been doing this for a few years now. It all began with two fortuitous events. The first was that he ran out of money to hire proper test pilots. The second was the foolhardy decision, on my part, to break into the back of his lab at night to sleep.

"No, no, no! That's not right. You have to turn it counter-clockwise!" Yeah, that's right. I was a vagrant. Or, if you prefer a more politically correct term, I was a woman experiencing homelessness. As I told you before, it's been a long time since I have been called by my full family name – or enjoyed the benefits attached to it. But like I said, that's a story for another time.

"Two minutes to go. Are you okay in there?" Have I mentioned that Bob was a good man? Every time we attempted this "launch" he was worried about my well-being. Not that there was anything to worry about. The "time machine" was just a rectangular mess of wires. Imagine one of those old standing medicine cabinets with a frame of metal closed in by transparent glass all around. Now, imagine it big enough to fit a couple of human beings inside and replace the glass with wire mesh. That was Bob's time machine. A glorified Faraday cage.

"Remember, the most important thing is to keep all your body parts and equipment inside the frame of the machine. Only what is inside it, including the frame itself, will dislocate through time – anything outside stays put. If it works … it could get really messy." That was the imperative word here: if. But I wasn't going to say anything. After all, this was part of our deal: Food and a roof for my test-pilot services.

"One minute to go. I'm feeling really good about this one. The thirty-first time might be the charm." I raised both my thumbs, and gave him a half-hearted smile, trying to keep both large military backpacks inside the metal frame. The one on my back held a huge battery, in case I got lost in the timestream and needed to activate the time machine myself. The one in front was loaded with all kinds of survival gear. After the twentieth trial (give or take), I told him I was happy to take my chances without them, but he would never allow it. He treated each attempt as if it was a definite thing.

"Remember," he said, his eyes bright and looking directly into mine, "if it works, you will jump five minutes into the future." Maybe next time, I'll find a way to drug him or something. Is there a drug that would knock him out for five minutes? At least then he'd feel like I'd jumped in time. It might put my "salary" at risk, but it would totally be worth it.

"…, 4, 3, 2, 1. Now!"

As was traditional, the last part of our routine was him pressing the big red button by the control panel. Then a blindingly bright light would explode all around as the generator pumped power into the Faraday cage. And then, just like the thirty times before this one, the machine burned every fuse and street transformer from here to the end of times, plunging us into total darkness.

———————— ⏳ ————————

Have you ever been thrown, fully dressed, into a deep, freezing swimming pool? Or what about a very, very hot one? That's about a tenth of what I felt.

I can't really say which sensation I felt first, as they all happened at the same time. The merciless pressure on my eardrums, almost imploding them. The hot, wet, sticky sensation – like cobwebs from hell – on my skin. The pungent smell of rotting vegetation mixed with a cornucopia of overripe fruits. And, worst of all, the drowning feeling of breathing densely heavy air.

At least I was still blinded from the time machine ignition, and was spared having the last of my senses overwhelmed. On the flip side, the absence of sight strongly contributed to my complete and utter despair.

As my vision slowly returned, my head spasmed agonizingly. It took me some time to realize that I had collapsed onto my knees – or I would have if it hadn't been for the two huge backpacks, which held me more or less upright inside the compact frame of Bob's time machine.

Now that I was starting to see again, not that I could see anything but some timid rays of light from above, my mind tried to make sense of what had happened.

That's when the weight of my military training finally paid off.

You remember my very classy family name, right? Well, while it's still not the moment for that story, this might be a good spot for a quick overview of my military years, which happened between that story and this one.

I never quite fit in to the military life, which I assume is not a big surprise to you.

I ended up spending most of my service in the Engineering Corps. It was actually bearable, and even, sometimes, enjoyable. I was in the Horizontal Construction unit, so wherever they needed something leveled, that's where I would go. I have to admit that bulldozing yourself through life is a catharsis to be envied.

And that mentality came back to me then: I had to bulldoze my way out of that darkness. Fighting against the drowning, the pressure, the heat, the smell – all those overpowering sensations, which had not subsided in any way. I rummaged around in the front backpack and found the hand-cranking flashlight. Even those simple movements made me feel exhausted. I turned it on.

Funny how it took some time for my brain to accept the obvious. Bob's time machine had finally worked. I will be honest, and I'm not ashamed to admit it – I was absolutely certain that the good professor had more than one screw loose. I was simply taking advantage of his delirious dreaming to make my own life a bit more bearable.

My very first thought when I turned on the flashlight was that somehow the lab had collapsed around us. Multi-colored stones surrounded most of the time cage. The rest, maybe a foot or so from the top, was buried under what I assumed was debris.

I tried to call for Bob, but my voice came out rough and weak. Then my mind processed what my eyes were seeing.

The lower part of the cage was not surrounded by stones; it was surrounded by stone, singular. A smooth, sheetlike vein of crystallized minerals, probably agate in the rough – the time machine had reentered the timestream inside a mountain, disintegrating or displacing the gemstone deposit previously occupying the same space.

I panicked. A cold shiver ran up and down my spine. Was I going to be the first human to trespass the barriers of time, just to be buried alive inside of a stone coffin? No. I had seen light. Where was it?

Pointing the flashlight upward, I could see where the stench of dying plants was coming from. The trail of light showed where the disintegrated rock gave way to a layer of soil, which in turn gave way to large leaves in different stages of decomposition, and between them, the feeble rays of sunlight. I was buried, but not completely.

It is an incredible piece of machinery, this human body of ours. Mine was already getting used to the new environment, and gradually I took some measure of control back from my senses. Wherever I was, the atmospheric pressure was higher than the lab, the air thicker, and the temperature much warmer.

I pulled myself up, inside the cage, and immediately started the procedures to activate the time machine again. That was why I was carrying the big battery on my back, anyway, in case something went wrong and I had to turn it back on. It was auto-configured to bring me back to the exact instant I left. Or at least, it was supposed to be.

The setup was very simple: a couple of cables, from each side of the backpack, needed to be attached to specific points on the metal frame. In a hip pack, attached to my left side, was the main CPU and the only controller that mattered: a big red button.

With everything set up, I reached for the button. That's

when the professor talked me out of it.

I would never admit it out loud, but spending years around a mad scientist, even a harmless one like Bob, ends up affecting you.

The only reason he hired test pilots, and then practically adopted a homeless vet like myself, was because he could not do the trip himself. He was too old, too fat, and, between his high blood pressure and his dodgy heart, too frail.

But what he had, in boatloads, to compensate for all that, was an extravagant passion about time travel and the unknowns of the past and future. He wanted, even through a proxy, to explore time. To visit famous past events, confirm conspiracy theories, watch the formation of nations, witness the death of martyrs, and take a peek at the posterity of humankind.

And in that instant between reaching for and pressing the red button, I decided to pay back the good professor. I would explore wherever and whenever I was, and I would bring him back a token of his success.

The professor had actually put a lot of thought into this time machine thing. Every side of the wire cage, including both floor and ceiling, had separate hinges and latches, which allowed me to simply open the top of it as if it was the lid of a box. Even smarter, the hinges were set up to open inward, which was especially useful in my situation.

A waterfall of leaves and dirt fell into the cage and onto me. But now I could finally see up there. It was some kind of dense tropical forest, with trees of all sizes and shapes laced with vines, fruits, berries, and endless leaves.

I left the heavy backpack with the battery inside and used the wire mesh of the cage itself as a ladder to climb up and out of it.

The view was amazing.

It was like being born again in a different world. I was standing on a forest floor, but I didn't recognize a single plant. They were all alien, weird, and larger than what I felt a forest should be. The buzzing and growling sounds of the local fauna were vivid and loud.

The air outside was much better than below ground, but the temperature was somehow even hotter. I couldn't fathom how such a humid place, protected from the sun by countless rows of plants, could be so scorching.

Plowing through my sweat, which was running down under my tactical clothing, I walked around. Obviously, I first closed and secured the lid of the time machine, covering it with foliage and planting four large sticks around its edges, so I would know where it was buried. I grabbed another stick to help me climb through the undergrowth.

The logical direction was uphill, as I needed to see as far as possible in the hope of identifying anything about where or when I was. I had landed on a slope, at what looked to be near the top of a mountain.

But, ironically enough, I did not have to reach higher ground to figure it out. I just had to look down, as a scuffling sound came closer, the leaves parted, and one part of my question was revealed.

The animal stopped at some distance, looking at me with

curious, bright eyes. It was as if some trickster god had morphed together a goose and a velociraptor. It was a biped, around three feet high, covered in dark brown feathers. It had small, taloned wings and a large, long tail that was also feathered. Its thick neck supported an equally thick, rounded beak that reminded me vaguely of a platypus.

I was definitely far, far in the past. Jurassic Park far.

The weird dinosaur, which I later discovered was called a Bambiraptor (I'm not kidding, go Google it), opened its beak wide – showing off about a thousand razor-sharp teeth, obviously – and emitted a high-pitched shrill. From all around came replies to its call. In surprise, I momentarily lost eye contact with it. Which was its cue to attack me.

Pure reflex and luck allowed me to swat the open Bambiraptor maw aside with the makeshift walking stick I'd been using to climb the hill. I saw leaves moving behind the dizzied animal and I knew more were coming.

I ran downhill, cursing the professor and looking for the four sticks marking the entrance to the time machine. There were plenty of prehistoric plants and soil already inside to take back as trophies; they would have to be enough.

Hope left me even before it could take hold. I found the machine – and two more of the beasts, who were scratching at the hatch of the wire cage. At least I would die knowing that my scent was apparently very pleasant to them.

I kept my momentum and continued downhill, deviating away from the two newcomers to the much-sought-after, never-before-tasted Homo sapiens buffet. All feelings of awe and even sensory overload were forgotten in the more pressing race for survival.

My arms and face were being slowly slashed apart by the foliage I was running into, but I couldn't stop. I had no idea where I was going, but I couldn't take the time to think. And as I was not thinking, I did not see the ravine.

Have you ever run toward a swimming pool and kept running even after you splashed into the water? Now imagine there is no water. That's exactly how it felt.

The tenths of a second floating in the air were followed by a hard impact and seemingly infinite rotations, as my body rolled down the leaf-covered ravine wall. A mesh of vines mercifully stopped me, hundreds of feet from my starting point.

I could still hear the Bambiraptors screeching, and I knew it was just a matter of time before they resumed the chase.

Groggily, I was looking around for something – I didn't know what – when I noticed a small natural cave at the foot of the ravine. Using all my remaining adrenaline, I got up and darted into it.

Thinking back now, this could have been the end of me. To run away from one danger, I foolishly entered a dark cave in a prehistoric jungle, without even considering what kind of dangers could lurk inside it.

Against all odds, no perils waited for me in the cave. It was narrow and irregularly shaped, which made it impossible, from only a few feet inside, to see out. But it was also quite shallow. So much so that even resting at the back of it, enough light came in to make a flashlight unnecessary. Not that I had the option anyway, as the trusty crank flashlight had been lost during my less-than-gracious descent.

Removing the backpack, I went straight for the canteen. Suddenly I imagined the old professor as a Boy Scout. That was the only logical explanation I could think of for the amount of survival gear he had packed.

As the adrenaline wore down, I realized I was sitting on some sharp things. I figured they were sticks, so I brushed my hand along the ground to clear a more comfortable sitting space.

That's when I realized that the sticks were actually bones and skulls. Not human, mind you, but nonetheless unsettling for someone in my situation. They must have been eaten a long time ago, because they were clean and gray, not even smelling of death.

There was this skull near me that seemed like a giant rodent, its hollow eyes and nostrils staring directly at me. At the exact instant I put my hand over it, intending to throw it far away, a familiar high-pitched screech echoed inside the cave. The sunlight undulated in shadows as the Bambiraptors moved in to finish me.

And now it's finally time to tell you about my family name.

My grandfather, the original Harold Archie Ladgrove, was a self-made millionaire, who bought his way into the highest level of society. My father, let's call him Hal 2.0, was born and raised in a world of smiling faces and vicious whispers, a world that accepted him for what he had, but not for who he was. His way of coping was to decide that he didn't want to be anything other than what he had.

At some point in time, I was born. His firstborn – a disappointing girl. Not what my dad had expected. Compounding that disappointment, my mother died in childbirth, and so I was also his onlyborn.

The most important thing my father had was his name. The legacy so hard-bought by my grandfather. He didn't contemplate what my name should be; it wasn't even a decision. That's how I became The Third.

This is where the story of my rebellious youth should go. How my father hated me, and how I made his life a living hell. But unfortunately, what actually happened was much worse.

Instead of rebelling against my name, I swallowed it. I let them wrap a boy's name around me, and carried it throughout my childhood. I allowed the kids at school to pile on every insult, every mockery they could come up with.

Instead of telling my father what a hypocrite he was, I let him dress me in expensive clothes he no longer had the means to pay for, and parade me in front of his 'friends' so he could fake the life he wished he still had.

Instead of screaming at the unfairness of not being properly loved and accepted by my own parent, I shrouded myself in sorrow. I stayed quiet; I stayed inconspicuous. I suffocated myself in the role of a permanent shrinking violet to keep from bothering him.

My only outward sin, from my father's point of view, was my military career. It was the only choice I saw that would allow me to get far away from everything I'd grown up with, and that he could not publicly deny me. After all, it was an honorable choice.

It's not hard to connect the dots from there to where I'd been yesterday. I was not experiencing homelessness. I had always been homeless.

As the dinosaurs, growling excitedly, approached me in single-file (they had to, given the narrowness of the cave), I experienced the cliché of seeing my whole life pass before me. And for the first time – despite being displaced in time and space – I didn't feel homeless. I felt angry.

If I died here and now, millions of years in the past, Bob would never know he wasn't a failure. Bob would never know he had been more of a father to me in two years than I had ever had in my life. He'd never know that the best moments of my life had been our breaks between tests, when his excitement and enthusiasm had me dreaming my own dreams for the first time, had me thinking that maybe I was brave enough to fight for them.

My right hand closed on the rodent's skull. My left hand grabbed for the nearest bone. A sound welled out of me – a sob? a battle cry? – and I jumped up. I ran forward, screaming death upon the dinosaurs.

No, not the dinosaurs.

Each swing of the gray skull, teeth first, ripped into a playground bully. Each strike of the bone tore through an indifferent glance, a disappointed sigh. Each head-butt, bite and kick rent apart my silent, lonely submissiveness.

Each inch conquered toward the light, in a frenzy of bones, feathers, and blood, was one step out of my own cocoon of silent suffering.

The blows took on a cadence, a rhythm of blossoming death, until only life was left. My life. A new life. As I reached the entrance of the cave, covered in blood, I celebrated with a howl so savage it didn't sound human.

I don't know what happened with the dinosaurs, because I

never looked back. Not even for the backpack, which I left inside the cave.

As if on cue, a torrential downpour began while I climbed back up the ravine. It rinsed me clean of the worst of the gore. It felt like it rinsed me down to the soul. I was still holding the skull, now badly damaged, and the bone, broken and split. They became makeshift climbing claws to help me ascend.

Once back on the forest floor, it was easy to follow my tracks to the time machine. My path looked like a triceratops had plowed through a wheat field.

In short order I was back where I had started. That was when I realized how badly injured I was: I was covered in open, bleeding gashes, some with broken teeth still embedded in my skin. But I couldn't stop just yet.

I cleared the way to the top hatch and opened it once more. I threw the skull and the bone inside before lowering myself, painfully, into the wire cage. The battery backpack was already attached to the frame of Bob's machine, and the hip pack was sitting calmly on top of it.

There was enough evidence of my trip inside the cage to prove to the good professor that it was all real, not a figment of my imagination. I put on the hip pack and pressed the red button without further ceremony.

Only one thought passed through my mind. The machine had been programed to jump just five minutes into the future, and had malfunctioned the first time. I really hoped it would malfunction the same way this time, and bring me back to where I'd started.

Otherwise, it would be a very long journey back if I had to make the jumps five minutes at a time.

Time for Everything

*"There is a time for everything,
and a season for every activity
under the heavens."*

—Ecclesiastes 3:1

"AND WHAT ABOUT ABOVE THE HEAVENS?"
Little Jack was standing on his pew, raising his hand and speaking clearly, as he had been taught to do when he had a question. "Do angels also have a time for each thing? Are there seasons in heaven?"

There were murmurs and a few giggles from the startled congregation in the small, dark nave. The preacher frowned in displeasure, stopping mid-sentence to deliver a stern look that included both the young boy and his parents.

"Yes. There are."

Little Jack jumped, startled. Out of nowhere, a well-dressed boy had appeared in the middle of the aisle, standing mere inches away from him. The boy – or was it a girl? – was not much taller than little Jack but seemed quite a bit older.

"But as to your first question, no, we don't have a time for each thing. We have time for everything."

"Who the hell are you?" little Jack blurted, too loudly. He instantly regretted using that word in this place, and cringed slightly in expectation of another stern look.

"No, again. Not hell. Heaven. I am Angel."

Little Jack was about to reply that even if he was young, he was not fool enough to believe in angels. But it was at that moment he realized he'd never gotten that second stern look … because the first one had never ended. The preacher, his parents, and everyone else around him were absolutely paralyzed, frozen in time. Even the book he had inadvertently knocked off the pew when he was startled was floating, pages mid-turn, in the air.

"Well, you don't have to believe me," said the boy, as though little Jack had voiced his thought. "But I am a time angel, and I am here to guide you through your time journey."

"You don't look like an angel."

"Have you ever seen an angel?"

"Sure, plenty of times."

"I don't mean in cartoons, or drawings, or movies. Have you ever seen an angel in real life?"

"No."

"I rest my case."

"What?"

"Never mind. Let's get moving. Stopping time is not a straightforward thing, even for angels."

"I thought angels would be taller …."

"What was that?"

"Nothing."

"Good, good. We begin yesterday."

Angel took little Jack's hand, and life rewound itself. They walked backward down the wooden boards of the church aisle, out onto the street, and into their family car as his mom unopened the door for him. Everything continued backward until they reached the night before, when he was laying down in his backyard, looking up at the stars.

"Does it really matter what happens up there?" Angel asked, laying down beside little Jack on the lawn, his head resting on his folded arms.

"The grown-ups say it does."

"It doesn't. What matters is what happens here." Angel touched little Jack's forehead and the sky exploded in motion. The celestial dome sped up, constellations crisscrossing over and over as planets danced around them in their continuously laced paths. Tens, hundreds, thousands of sunsets followed sunrises, while millions more sunrises backtracked into sunsets – not always in that order.

Little Jack has the bird dead center in his sling's aim and shoots. The lifeless bird topples from its nest, bringing down with it a half-opened egg with a hatchling inside. In another sunrise, the stone is not thrown, and a pair of beaks will tweet, joyful.

Teen Jack freezes and chooses not to ask her to the prom. He is the only one alone, shy and miserable in the corner of the room. In another sunset, the request is accepted, and by God, there'll be dancing.

Jack is being scolded by his very first boss for arriving late again. He opts to answer back, angrily. In another sunrise, he listens and will keep this job and others after.

Jack is not sure he wants to know the truth, but he confronts her anyway. She confesses, and he watches as she cries. The betrayal is painfully real. He looks deep into her eyes before turning around and leaving, rage growing with each step. In another sunset, he chooses forgiveness and there will be mending.

Middle-aged Jack holds the check in both hands, looking once more at the tempting zeros before ripping it apart. The loan is too risky; his dream will have to wait. In another sunrise, he uses the seed money and the bet on himself will pay off, many times over.

Old Jack vows to hold her hand until she comes back to him, forever if necessary. The hum of the machines, as rhythmic as the hospital bills, becomes the soundtrack of his life. In another sunset, a tough decision will bring them both peace.

Little Jack decides to not raise his hand. He lets the question die inside of him. In another sunrise, he will laugh, cry, and dream of unwritten futures under a starry sky.

"And that's it. I hope you enjoyed the ride," Angel said, disappearing. The preacher's stern gaze deepened at the sound of the book clattering noisily onto the wooden floor.

The startled congregation, lit by the ruby hues of the afternoon sun through the stained glass, finally reacted to the interruption, muttering and whispering. The preacher, shifting his stance on the marble tiles, was at a loss for words.

Jack didn't care. His mission had been accomplished; he had asked the question. Lowering his wrinkled, sun-spotted hand, old Jack walked out of his pew, down the aisle, and out into the world.

Better Luck Next Time

"BATTLE STATIONS, report!" the lustrously bald Captain shouts, as a particularly nasty proton torpedo explosion rocks the bridge of the starship TSS Interperion.

"Lower starboard sub-light engines not responding, sir," the Helm Officer replies, trying his best to maneuver the Interperion with only five engines remaining.

"Widespread casualties in decks two through eighteen, and extensive hull breach on deck thirty-one, sir," the Species Resources Officer responds.

"Disphasor banks almost depleted, sir. Force shields decaying at triple rate speeds, currently at fifteen percent," the Tactical Officer stoically states.

"Science, what are our odds?" the Captain asks, knowing that his Science Officer would not speak unless a question was specifically directed at her.

"Our odds of survival are below two-and-a-half percent,

Captain. May I suggest we immediately execute the contingency plan?" the Science Officer coldly suggests.

"Damn! I thought the seventh time would be the charm." The Captain rises from his central chair on the bridge. "Well, let's NOT try our fortunes to the last man. Whose turn is it?"

"Not me. I just went," the Helm Officer is quick to assert.

"I'm not even in the schedule anymore, remember?" The Tactical Officer tapped his HESOR (Hearing Equipment and Sensory Organ Replacement). "Too much time sickness. I'm practically useless for a whole day." The Tactical Officer didn't need to remind anyone, as more than one of them are already edging as far away from him as possible, noses twisted at the faint scent of vomit that still clings to him.

The Science Officer tilts her head to the side, as if she is about to say something.

"The lady does not protest enough, methinks," Captain shouts. "You don't need to wait for a question to talk. You're the Science Officer, damn it!"

The Science Officer just tilts her head to the other side and raises an eyebrow – her version of cringing at yet another Shakespeare misquote. But despite the Captain's scolding, he's failed to directly question her.

The starship rocks again, as yet another blast hits them dead center, causing lights to flicker and sparks to fly all around the bridge.

"Fine! What do you want to say?" the Captain finally asks, completely regretting accepting a crew member from planet Molten V, and wondering how an entire society could survive if they always had to wait for a direct question to communicate.

"I believe, sir," the Science Officer says, nodding at the scrawny young junior officer standing at the outskirts of the bridge, "that it is Ensign Fletcher's turn."

Ensign's Private Log, spacedate 45652.2:

We are heading into another probable battle against the V'tors Federation, as we are crossing through the neutral zone, again. I have no idea why – it's classified. But today, I'll be there. It will be my first assignment on the bridge.

It's exciting. I would never hope for disaster, but if something bad should happen (and keep happening again and again), I could end up being chosen to save the ship.

The odds are extremely low, of course, since I'll be last in line for the contingency plan – but who knows, right? I may be the first Ensign to ever travel back in time.

Fletcher runs through the partially destroyed corridors of the Interperion, passing through the acrid smell of burning plexi-plastic and jumping over his dying crewmates, until he reaches the timeporter room.

He holds the weirdly shaped doorknob, actually the only door in the ship with a knob, and feels a slight sting as the needle perforates his skin. This is the only room that still employs a local-scan physical-DNA lock, the most secure lock ever built.

The timeporter room is a smaller version of a standard transporter room, with only one pad. The Interperion is the first and only ship of the USSE (the Unified Solar Systems Empire), to contain the Singularity Timeloop Grid Machine, or STiGMa.

The STiGMa is the pinnacle achievement of the whole combined brain powers of the USSE. Scientists had finally figured out the math behind time traveling to the past. And it was actually very simple. The only hitch was that for each trip in time, a machine would require the equivalent output energy of a singularity implosion.

When presented with this dilemma, the USSE Engineer Corps came up with a straightforward solution. They just built the time machine attached to the anti-matter reactor of a starship engine. To activate the STiGMa, one simply had to self-destruct the starship with a matter-anti-matter implosion, which would create the needed singularity power output to travel back in time. Hence the STiGMa name.

Not that Ensign Fletcher is thinking about any of that. He is focused on not failing his Captain or his shipmates.

He enters the small room, going straight for the control panel totem, and presses the pre-configured big red button on the screen. The hexagonal timeporter pad lights up with a purplish hue and a ship-wide countdown begins.

"Timeloop Grid initiated," the female voice of the ship's computer announces. "Matter-anti-matter engine singularity in T-minus 5 seconds, starting now. 5 … 4 …"

The Ensign tumbles toward the timeporter pad. The ship lurches violently again, but he holds himself steady in the right position.

"3 … 2 … 1."

Silence.

Fletcher is somewhat underwhelmed, maybe even disappointed. The time traveling experience was not what he'd expected. Between a single blink of his eyes, all the blaring sirens and shaking walls have been replaced by the silent, empty interior of the timeporter room. The only evidence that he's come from a disastrous future is the lingering burning smell on his skin, and the absence of all his clothes.

"Computer, what's the current spacedate and spacetime?"

"It is spacetime 14:31 of spacedate 45652.2," replies the intentionally comforting voice.

Exactly as planned, he's traveled back in time six Earth hours. Whoever set up the standard time travel loop decided that six hours would be a good amount of time to alter whatever disaster caused the ship to auto-destruct.

"Computer, where in space is the Interperion relative to the border of the V'tors Federation neutral zone, from the USSE side?" Fletcher asks. He is trying to get some bearing on their situation.

"The Interperion is 0.8 light-years inside the neutral zone, from the USSE border limit."

They have already crossed into the neutral zone, so short of running away and embarrassing the whole USSE, there is no avoiding a fight. Fletcher needs to get to the Captain as soon as possible. But before that, he has a grim cleaning task.

The Ensign opens a metal locker, the only furniture in the spartan room, and removes a bio-disphasor rifle from it.

"Computer, locate Ensign Fletcher."

"Ensign Fletcher is in his quarters, on deck twenty-seven." The computer is not reporting the location of the time-dislocated Ensign Fletcher, but the badge his past self is wearing, the one all personnel have to wear at all times, including when they shower.

Recollection hits Fletcher. He is getting ready to go to the bridge, finishing his daily log.

"Computer, execute emergency point-to-point transport of Ensign Fletcher following Timeloop protocol, authorization Gamma-Gamma-Delta-Omega-Two."

Inside Ensign Fletcher's quarters, an unsuspecting junior officer is just finishing his log, "… I could be the first Ensign to ever travel back in time," when the bright tingling of a transporter beam dematerializes him.

Ensign Fletcher from the past, rematerialized on the hexagonal pad of the timeporter room, stares down the barrel of a bio-disphasor rifle being held by a naked version of himself. An hours-older version of himself.

"We were!" Time traveling Ensign Fletcher fires the rifle, on its maximum setting, completely disintegrating his younger self.

Ensign Fletcher runs through the pristine, lavender-scented corridors of The Interperion, getting annoyed looks from the highly disciplined crew as he passes by.

He is going through the protocol in his head, and so far everything has been perfect. He arrived naked in the past, bio-disintegrated himself, got the clothes and badge of his past self, and put the rifle back in the locker. No paradoxes to deal with; well, at least no paradoxes involving his past self.

Ensign Fletcher is the last one to arrive on the bridge. The First Officer is starting on a reprimand when he shouts. "Timelooped Ensign Fletcher, reporting for duty, sir."

"What the frack?" blurts the First Officer. Other, more

colorful expressions come from the other bridge officers, except for the Science Officer, who, of course, does not react at all.

"Report, Ensign," the Captain orders.

"In approximately six hours, we will face three battlecruisers from the V'tors Federation, and we will lose the battle. Badly. I was eighth in line in the contingency plan."

"Seven times? We've failed seven times already?" The First Officer is aghast at the prospect.

"Senior officers to the Ready Room. Tactical, you have the conn," commands the Captain, standing up and stretching. "Shall we?" he asks Ensign Fletcher with a smile.

Fletcher's excitement at being in the Ready Room for the first time rapidly dissolves into a sense of incredulity. He'd been expecting an intensive and repetitive debriefing from the Captain and the other officers, but he'd barely told his story once when the Captain interrupted him with a 'brevity is the soul of wit' quote. Then a pointless discussion about the timeloop protocol erupted.

None of them seem to be worried about their certain deaths at the hands of a superior enemy in just a few hours. They don't seem worried because they are not. They're like a bunch of video game players discussing their last saved game. At some point in the meeting, someone asks Fletcher what their vector of entrance into the enemy territory had been in the previous future timeline. Then the Captain simply picks another one, apparently at random, and orders everyone back to the bridge.

The Ensign's station, at the back of the bridge, allows

him a full view of everyone. And in those uneventful hours navigating deeper into the neutral zone, Fletcher realizes something that he missed the first time, despite having a sense it had been the same in the previous timeline.

Every single one of the senior officers is just going through the motions, in complete apathy. The spark of discovery, the stress of anticipating battle, the dread of possible doom – they aren't present in the bridge at all. Even when Tactical reports the approach of two enemy battlecruisers and the Captain turns on the Red Alert, there is no rush of adrenaline on the bridge.

How many battles had the senior officers won, just because they knew exactly what had happened before? How many surprises had been rendered completely innocuous by knowing what was ahead of them? How many timeloops must have happened before the Captain, an icon for the USSE Startroopers, simply decided to not care any longer?

Sure enough, a third battlecruiser shows up in the sensors, flanking them in a very familiar configuration.

It's not that the Interperion's officers don't fight back. It's that they don't really care if they win or lose. They know that they will have another chance if everything goes wrong. Which certainly looks to be the case. Again.

"Science, what are our odds?" the Captain asks.

"Our odds of survival are ten percent, Captain. Should we execute the contingency plan?" the Science Officer asks nonchalantly.

"Nah. Let's wait for 'the gloomy shade of death,' shall we? Who's next in line for the contingency plan?" The Captain looks around to see the reluctant hand of the First Officer going up.

Between sparks from localized explosions and the

rocking of the Interperion under enemy proton fire, Ensign Fletcher's mind is racing. This was not why he joined the USSE Startroopers. He doesn't want to become a mindless executor of past strategies of failed futures. He wants to explore the universe, in awe of the unexpected. He wants to live every day as if it could be his last, even while he hopes it won't be.

An explosion erupts on the starboard side of the bridge, knocking down a couple of junior officers. No senior officer moves to call the Medic; most don't even spare them a glance. But Fletcher sees the Captain look at them with what he can only describe as … envy.

That's a bridge too far for him.

Fletcher doesn't have to stealthily sneak off of the bridge. No one notices or misses him.

As soon as the interdeck lift's doors slide open, the disenchanted Ensign once again runs through wrecked, charred, and bloody corridors to reach the timeporter room. He doesn't even register the sting of the secure lock's needle.

He gets inside, closes the door, and goes straight for the weapons locker, quickly firing at the door's lock – guaranteeing he won't be disturbed. No way back. It's in his hands now.

Fletcher stands by the control panel totem and dismisses the pre-configured settings. He pauses a few seconds to recall his previous day, trying to remember when he last went to bed. A familiar curse, loud enough to be heard over the Red Alert and through the titanium door, comes from the First Officer, followed by the unmistakable sound of a hand disphasor. Fletcher quickly reprograms the timeloop and presses the reconfigured red button.

The hexagonal timeporter pad lights up with a purplish hue and a ship-wide countdown begins.

"Timeloop initiated," the female voice of the ship's computer announces. "Anti-matter engine collapse in T-minus 5 seconds, starting now."

"5 …"

Ensign Fletcher loses his footing as the anti-inertia field flickers under a barrage of enemy shelling.

"… 4 …"

The timeporter room begins to glow orange and then red as the disphasor blast melts a small hole through the door.

"… 3 …"

Fletcher crawls onto the lit platform.

"… 2 …"

A pair of angry eyes shows through the newly-made hole. "Don't you dare, Fletcher. I will kill you!" the First Officer sputters.

"… 1."

Silence.

"Computer, what's the current spacedate, spacetime, and the Interperion's position relative to the V'tors Federation neutral zone?" a naked and slightly smoking ensign Fletcher commands.

"It is spacetime 23:00 of spacedate 45651.9, and the Interperion is 1.7 light-years from the neutral zone, still in USSE space," replies the steady computerized voice.

Perfect. He's done it. If he follows his plan, at least the

Captain will have enough time to make an actual choice. But should Fletcher follow his plan? Now that he is once again in the safety of the near past, looking at the spotless walls of the timeporter room, his idea seems less reckless and more totally crazy.

Suddenly he is self-conscious of his trembling hands and the sweat rolling down his exposed body. The whole idea made much more sense a few minutes ago – or rather, almost a day in the future. Now it sounds wrong, almost mutinous. Certainly murderous.

Not that he has to follow his ill-conceived plan. To all intents and purposes, he still has done nothing wrong. Or, more accurately, no one would be the wiser that he's jumped back to the past out of turn. Shouldn't he give them all another chance? What if what he witnessed was just an anomaly? What if he misinterpreted the whole situation?

Picking up the rifle from the weapons locker, he gets ready to disintegrate himself again. He will try once more. Maybe this time, with more hours to prepare, events will take a different turn.

Events definitely take a different turn. He alerted the crew, but this time, with almost one full day of advantage, the senior officers are even less worried. They even throw an impromptu party for the battle to come. And when the fight does come, they are not only apathetic – they are hung over.

Ensign Fletcher regrets not taking action the first time. Well, if at first you don't have the balls to do it, go back in time and explode them all.

"3 … 2 … 1 …"

Silence.

"It is spacetime 11:00 of spacedate 45652.2, and the Interperion is 1.7 light-years from the neutral zone, still in USSE space," the faithful computer replies, as a naked Ensign Fletcher reaches for the toolbox in the weapons locker.

He opens the panels under the timeporter's hexagonal pad and searches for the Fluorite gemstones. Several shards of this precious crystal are used to keep the timeporter from overheating. There are obviously several layers of redundancy, and disabling all its conduits and connections takes a fair amount of time. But a couple of hours does the trick.

Fletcher goes to the control panel and looks at the red button. This is going to hurt, a lot. He presses the red button. For the last time. Ever.

"Completely destroyed, every single fluorite prism is destroyed." The Chief Engineer's statement brings horror and denial to the faces of all the senior crew, except for the Science Officer, of course. "Nothing short of a complete reassembling of the STiGMa, with the ship in a dry dock, could bring it back online. We are stuck in the regular time flow."

The Captain looks at the central tactical hologram of the ready room, showing the Interperion about to cross into the Neutral Zone in less than an hour. "Once more, Mr. Fletcher. What happened?"

"Yes, sir." A hastily dressed and still barefoot Ensign complies, noting that this time there is no mention of brevity. "In about ten hours we will engage multiple hostile ships from the V'tors Federation, I don't know how many as I was not at the bridge."

"Why not?" the First Officer asks, his tone skeptical. "Why would you miss your first-ever bridge shift?"

"Like I said before, sir, I, uh, had a serious, well, intestinal problem, sir. So, I asked to be replaced, and I just stayed in my quarters, until I heard the call for battle stations. By that time I was feeling better, and was running toward my lower deck station, when the black alert came on." Fletcher keeps checking the reactions on everyone's faces. The black alert meant all senior officers had been killed or disabled, and any remaining officer should try to reach and activate the STiGMa. "I was the first to arrive at the STiGMa, but the computer was already in the final seconds of its auto-destruct countdown, so I got in, changed the timeloop timeframe and activated it. As soon as I blinked into the past, I was thrown from the pad by several micro explosions. When I collected myself, I came straight here, sir."

"But why did you change the standard six hours?" the Captain asks.

"I was afraid, sir. I didn't know what had happened. It was a split-second decision to buy us some more time. I apologize, sir."

The Captain looks back at the tactical hologram. "No apologies needed, Ensign. 'Better ten hours too soon than a minute too late.' You have not only saved us all, but you have given us what may be our last prescient choice. Now, to the sick bay with you. If you have no serious injuries, I need you back on the bridge, on the double. And don't worry about the other Fletcher, I've already dispatched a team to take care of him." The Captain, turning away from Fletcher, looks at his senior crew. A long-lost spark of defiance comes into his eyes as he utters his next words.

"Timeloopers die many times before their deaths; the valiant never taste death but once." And for the first time in a long while, none of the senior crew cringes at their captain's misquoting. Not even the Science Officer.

Ensign's Private Log, spacedate 45652.3:

The Captain has just issued a ship-wide communication. The Interperion will venture forth into the Neutral Zone, even without the STiGMa. I know what awaits us and I have no regrets. Actually, I'm excited. I can finally see – in the timbre of the Captain's voice and the sharp reactions of each senior officer – what inspired me to join the Startroopers. And as the Captain will surely mention at some point during the battle to come, 'a sentient being can die but once.'

Tempus Pompeius

"IMPOSSIBLE! This just makes no sense." Clive spoke aloud to himself, alone in the lab.

The ancient dead woman had already been remarkable, even before her DNA results came back. Unlike most of the other plaster casts from the ruins of Pompeii, which showed people in their last instants of despair and agony, specimen L318 seemed to be almost at peace when she was caught under the furious hot ashes and poisonous fumes of the erupting Mount Vesuvius. The old lady, according to the CT scans of her bones, was found comfortably sitting on a stone bench, legs crossed beneath her, chin resting in both hands – as if she was meditating – when her end came. On her lap sat a half-eaten, carbonized loaf of bread.

The bread itself was not that strange, considering she was found inside what would have been a bakery of ancient Pompeii; the strangeness was that she was utterly alone. Not only the bakery, but all the houses and shops near where she was found were empty – they contained no human remains.

But that was not why Clive was rechecking her DNA analysis again and again. He was redoing it because, for all genetic intents and purposes, this ancient, elderly, dead woman was his daughter.

Clive had been comparing his own DNA out of boredom, as a kind of treasure hunt through time to find any shared DNA traces between himself and those millennia-old samples.

Not that he should have been doing it in the first place, but he was so frustrated with his current, unreasonable assignment that he no longer cared. The lead researcher was lazy and never in the mood to work, so Clive was basically in charge of all the DNA analysis. And since he could, why not also analyze his own DNA?

From there it was just too much temptation not to compare his own chromosomes with those of the ancient people. Somewhere in the back of his mind, he hoped to find some residual traces of a DNA sequence, and dream about a rich and powerful ancestor. Maybe to find some sliver of connection in his otherwise directionless life.

He did not expect this, though. A 49.8% match. Forty-nine point eight percent of his chromosomes were an exact match with those found in the bones of this old woman's remains from over two thousand years ago.

The only logical conclusion was that the sample had somehow become contaminated when he first opened it for study. He could not fathom how, but it was the only possibility. From his many professional failures, Clive had at least learned one thing: If something goes wrong, be the first to explain, not the last to get the blame.

Clive collected his laptop, notebooks, and any other evidence of his genetic shenanigans he could find, and dumped them all in his backpack. He left the refrigerated, sterile environment of the makeshift lab for the hot, humid, and dusty streets of Pompeii's excavation site. He was running toward the main administrative building, to tell his boss what had happened, when he realized the ever-present tourists were nowhere to be seen. Clive, already melting under the scorching Italian summer sun, checked his smart watch and saw it was late in the afternoon. Nobody would be around until tomorrow.

At that moment, standing at an age-old crossroads in a ghost city, he decided tomorrow was too far in the future, and that he needed answers today.

Finding the exact location of specimen L318 proved to be a challenge. Despite his fancy title of Genetic Archeologist, Clive's total actual archeological experience could be summed up to two of those toy dinosaur excavation kits he'd given his nephew, where he'd helped him dig plastic fossils out of fake rock.

This was just one more gig in his endless journey through professions, and he already knew he still hadn't found his true vocation. He'd first thought technology was his thing, but he never even finished his electrical engineering major. He tried computer science, but programing for too long bored him. He'd decided to switch to a pure science, and had barely managed to get his diploma in chemistry. At least that degree had helped him to jump from job to job until this current opportunity showed up. He thought it would be great because it required his unique combination of skills. But a week into the job, he'd already become so disinterested that he'd hardly paid attention to the basic archeology training.

So when he opened the toolbox in the excavation site, he had no idea what he should use. He grabbed two tools that looked like a hammer and a very thin chisel. He wanted to collect another sample himself, to run more tests (which, if he were thinking straight, would have been the last thing to do if he believed he had contaminated the first sample).

He finally found the eerie plaster cast of the dead old woman. It was positioned indifferently on a metal table, with a note saying it was scheduled for another, more detailed CT scan.

Clive examined the plaster body and decided to open a small hole in the back of the head, to try and get some material from the spine of this alleged daughter. He positioned the chisel and tapped lightly with the hammer. Nothing happened. He tapped again, a tad harder. Still nothing. He hammered once more, now with force. The plaster sheared in a neat line, and the head popped clean off of the torso, unceremoniously rolling free over the ground until it was stopped by a nearby box. The plaster covered eyes, accusingly, stared straight at Clive.

Severed head in hand, Clive tried to at least make it stay put on top of the plaster body. One more broken piece of plaster would not be strange in the archeological site, but a beheaded specimen would definitely cost him much more than his job. The problem was that something was jutting from the neck area, preventing the head from balancing.

It was some kind of necklace the woman had been

wearing when she was buried in ashes. Clive's hammering must have dislocated it from within. He pulled the metal chain, and out of the plaster it came, bringing with it a large rectangular pendant.

He rubbed his hand over the pendant, clearing the residual plaster, and saw a gem-inlaid, metallic surface. Curiosity piqued, he continued to clean it, and to his utter shock, he held in his hand what appeared to be a slightly open mechanical pocket watch. He fully opened the lid, revealing it was less of a watch and more of an astrolabe. Even more astounding, the complex pieces of clockwork inside the rectangular astrolabe were in full movement.

Clive froze for a few moments, mesmerized by the tiny revolutions of small cogs and the yo-yoing of miniature springs. He was not able to fully come to terms with the last few hours, and did not know what to do – or even think – next.

Out of reflex more than anything, or maybe just to stop the hypnotizing effect of the open astrolabe, he removed the remaining dirt from the lid's edge, and closed it.

Clive, the plaster body beheader, would never be seen again. At least, in his own time.

"When I closed this lid," Clive – or rather Clivius Pistoribus, his adopted name in the ancient Roman Empire – explained to his ten-year-old daughter, "I instantly appeared inside the terma del Foro, in the middle of the male frigidarium." He repeated the motion on the gem-inlaid pendant he wore at all times, snapping it shut with a click.

"Why didn't you try to use it again to go back to your own time?" an excited Aelia, Clivius' daughter, asked her dad in heavily Latin-accented, but otherwise perfect, English.

"I desperately tried," Clivius honestly replied, feeling a pang of guilt. "But if it had worked, I wouldn't have had you, would I?" Lines crinkled at the edges of his eyes, which were lit with happiness. It was his usual expression. "Anyway, see those small pieces? They were all moving when I first opened it. After I arrived here, they never moved again. I pushed all its buttons and turned all its knobs, with no effect."

"Then what?" Aelia pressed.

"It was the middle of the night, around the end of the secunda vigilia, so nobody was in the terma, or anywhere else for that matter. It was a warm night with a full moon. After the initial shock – and almost being caught by one of the watchers as I walked aimlessly, and open-mouthed, through the streets of a living and breathing Pompeii – I ran back to the terma. I found some clothes and sandals, to both dress myself as a local, and to hide my modern clothes and future stuff. I had to be inconspicuous."

"Right. First rule of time travel: blend in," Aelia completed. This wasn't her dad's first story about time travel. She had heard all about the horseless carriage of Marty McFly, the exterminator golem from the future, and the star travelers who rescued the last whales on Earth (or something like that).

"Right. Not that I had it all sorted out in my head, at that time. I didn't believe it was real." Clivius smiled at his captivated daughter, and continued, "I had been working for a few months in Pompeii – in the future, I mean – so I had learned some Italian. That, in conjunction with a few Latin words from all my years of science studies, allowed me to pass by as a peregrinus, and not starve to death."

Tough memories flooded back to Clivius, as he thought about those early days in the past. His most recurring terror, after he had come to terms with the fact he had time traveled, was the fear of being buried alive under the ashes of Vesuvius. He'd tried to ask around, after he'd improved his Latin enough, to find out what year he'd landed in, but years in that period followed a regnal calendar. Discovering he was in the "fifth year of Claudius Germanicus" helped little, since he knew almost nothing about ancient Roman emperors and their reigns in the modern calendar years.

This specific dread had only disappeared when Aelia was born. After four pregnancies and two living sons, he'd finally had a daughter. Now his fear was a different one. He was safe, as he knew the remains found in the future were of a woman in her late eighties. Therefore, he must have traveled back many decades before the infamous volcanic explosion. But what about Aelia's future?

He did not share those thoughts, though. They would bring up some very uncomfortable questions, and he was not ready for them. Instead, he continued the story with something he knew would distract his daughter.

"The truth is that I only survived because of Lady Leda."

Aelia lit up upon hearing the name of the female merchant. She came to town once every year or two, and only stayed a few days. But she was one of Aelia's favorite people.

"Not a chance, Lady Leda. I'll hand it over after you tell me how you met my dad." Fourteen-year-old Aelia held back a loaf of fresh bread as ransom.

"Again? Fine, fine," Lady Leda, speaking strongly Britannia-accented Latin, conceded with an indulgent smile. "Give me my bread and walk with me. I will tell you all I can until we reach the Herculaneum Gate. Deal?"

"Deal."

The extraordinarily vivid old merchant woman put the bread into one of the side bags her donkey carried, and pulled the animal along the streets of Pompeii beside a radiant Aelia. Lady Leda took the longest way through the city, as she wanted to spend as much time as possible with her young protégé. She felt greedy for more time with this vibrant, happy child, even on her usual trips – and this time she knew it would be years until they met again.

Lady Leda's visits had become more and more important for Aelia. Her particular upbringing had not been very … traditional, by any Pompeian standards. Her dad would act as others did in public, but then would walk back almost everything to her in private, saying this or that custom was barbaric and that his daughter would not follow them. Aelia did not have many friends.

But for some reason, Lady Leda understood. She was the kind of woman who listened to Aelia, in a way no other person did. Without judgment.

"I first met your father over there, under one of those arches of the Macellum." Lady Leda pointed to the large structure, just northeast of the Forum, where the main marketplace of Pompeii was located. "I had just arrived from my travels and was minding my own business, having a very interesting conversation with my previous donkey, when Clivius approached me. He heard my accent and thought we spoke the same native language. Despite not recognizing most of the words coming from his mouth, I could understand what he wanted. Help."

They kept walking through the city, passing by the Forum Baths. "The biggest advantage of being a traveler is that you pick up things along the way – like languages, and a knack for identifying outsiders. Your father could not have been less *in*." Lady Leda smiled mischievously and Aelia giggled. "I took pity on him. I'd already decided to help him find some kind of job with one of the shop owners who used to buy my wares, when he showed me the sheets of white papyrus."

"Tell me more about the white papyrus," Aelia burst out, her excitement growing as the story finally arrived where she was expecting. She obviously knew all about the white papyrus, or paper, as her dad called it, and his claims he had brought it with him from the future. This was one of the reasons she still hadn't completely dismissed her father's stories. "Had you really never seen it before? Why is it so valuable? Where did he get it?"

"Again with this, eh?" Lady Leda looked back at Aelia, amused. "First, nothing has changed since the last time I told you. As far as I know, your dad is the only source of the white papyrus in the whole world right now. Second, you know why it is so valuable. Have you ever touched any other papyrus as soft, white, and thin as your father's? Do you have any idea what nobles and clerics would pay for just a few pieces of it? And finally, your father never told me how he got them, just that it was his inheritance from a faraway place he used to live. He never told me where."

"Okay. You may continue," Aelia said, jokingly fluttering her hand as she imagined a benevolent empress might.

"Oh, thank you, your majesty," Lady Leda replied in kind. "We struck a bargain. He would give me exclusivity on selling the white papyrus, and I would never tell anyone he was the source of it. In exchange, I would help him establish his life here in Pompeii, and find him an honest job."

"And that, I suppose, is how he met my mom?"

———————— ⧗ ————————

The fragrance of fresh baked bread was still Aelia's favorite smell, even after all these years working at the family bakery. She was a woman now, at sixteen, but her most treasured pastime was still kneading dough with her father. They didn't have to do it, of course. The success of Clivius' baked goods, after he'd inherited the bakery from his late father-in-law, had not only granted him full Roman citizenship but also made them reasonably wealthy for a plebeian family. They had enough slaves to work the mills, the oven, and all parts of the bread-making process.

But her father still loved to knead the dough. And she enjoyed doing it with him. It was also an opportunity for them to talk about anything and everything, always in English, to the despair of her mother and older brothers. The rest of the family not only didn't speak this unknown language, but were also of the opinion they shouldn't advertise too much the fact that Clivius was not of Pompeian birth.

"Where is she, dad? Another biennium is coming to an end; she should have been here already," Aelia said in obvious frustration.

"Don't worry, she always comes, doesn't she?" Clivius retorted. "I actually think she keeps coming back more for you than for my paper. I'm at the end of my supply, anyway."

"Right. And since you brought it from the future, there is no way to find more, right?"

"You know what?" he said, thumping down his mound of dough with determination. "I was going to wait until your birthday, but I have waited too long for this. It is past time to prove to you that your old man is not just a creative storyteller." Clivius cleaned his hands and called one of Aelia's brothers to take their place. "Come with me."

Their house was part of the same building as the bakery, but deeper inside the block and farther away from the noises of the merchant street. Clivius held Aelia's hand as he led her down into their basement.

There was one room in their house that nobody but Clivius was allowed to enter. It was behind a locked door – ironclad – at the very end of their subterranean cellar.

"Are you taking me in?" Aelia would not have been more incredulous if she had been asked to enter the inner sanctum of Apollo's temple.

"Yes. It is ready for you. Or better yet, you are ready for it."

Aelia was absolutely entranced by the small people, dressed in bizarre clothes, talking inside the rectangular glass. Her dad had explained the concept of a "movie," and showed her pictures appearing to move by flipping drawn-on parchment sheets rapidly, but in her mind they were still minuscule men stuck inside a dream glass.

She had always wanted to believe her dad's stories, as all girls want to unconditionally believe in their fathers. But deep in her soul, she actually thought he was a little crazy.

Not anymore.

The subterranean room, illuminated by traditional oil lamps, had all sorts of non-traditional contraptions sitting on top of a central table, and on several shelves around the walls. There was also a large coin chest embedded in the wall, with a metal lock and key, that would not have been cheap.

From one side of the rectangular magic glass, some strings were connected to a white cube, which in turn was connected to some more strings all wrapped around pieces of metal. More strings led to what looked like a well lever.

"This is called a smartphone," her father explained. "It needs electricity to function – the same thing lightning is made of." Clivius was dying to tell her all about the science behind it, and how it took him almost two decades to finally harness all the necessary materials and experiment with them until he succeeded in building a homemade, crank-powered generator, but he thought that best to leave to a later time.

Seeing the wonder in his daughter's eyes, Clivius was proud that his strange and varied science background had not gone to waste. This was worth all his false starts and failures.

"And this," he carried on, opening the coin chest in the wall, "is all the other stuff I brought with me from the future." He showed her his laptop, notebooks, earphones, smartwatch, and the many small things that populate a nerd's backpack.

"I used some of them, plus a lot of other materials that Lady Leda procured for me over the years, and my knowledge of future science to make this work. And this is why I insisted on your English education. I hoped, one day,

I could share this with you."

Aelia looked up at her dad. He had just been upgraded, in her mind, from possible madman and town weirdo to real-life time traveler.

Aelia spent years exploring every single thing on her dad's cellphone and laptop. He had lots of content "locally downloaded." There were books, music, comics books, movies, cartoons, games, and all kinds of apps. Nonetheless, her limitless source of sorrow was the phrase "No network connection, please try again." Her dad tried to explain time and again why he couldn't make this go away, but she never felt less frustrated.

She learned. From the news and podcast apps, she read and listened to dozens of news reports from the week her dad left the future. From the music app, she experienced unfathomable rhythms and sounds. Through the games she finally understood what a DeLorean was, saw an Enterprise, and played Dungeons and Dragons. And from a specific game called Civilization, she learned where she was in history. From a star app, she learned about planets and constellations. From a language app, she fell in love with and began to learn French. From the books – traditional, audio, and comic – she was introduced to life in different eras, and to fantastic characters like Wonder Woman, Sherlock Holmes, Princess Amethyst, Hank Spiros, Cinderella, and Drizzt Do'Urden.

What she liked the most, though, was reading her dad's letters in the apps mail, messages, and WhatsApp. It showed a version of him she did not expect: a drifting, self-centered, and unhappy one.

As the novelty of the electronics gradually diminished, her curiosity regarding the items in the locked coin chest increased. So much so, that one night she surreptitiously snuck the key from her dad's bedroom and spent the whole evening reading page after page of that incredibly smooth, white parchment her dad called paper.

That was the night she discovered the truth of how her dad had come into possession of the clockwork box. Literally over her dead body.

"There she is." Clivius nodded his head, one particularly hot morning, indicating an ancient-looking woman waving at them as she sat on a small cart, directing the donkey that pulled it.

Aelia, on the verge of her eighteenth year of life, cleaned her hands, grabbed a still-warm loaf of bread, and ran out of the bakery to hug Lady Leda.

"It's so good to see you!" Aelia took a step back in surprise. It had been a little more than a year since she last saw Lady Leda, but she had aged much since then. Her skin was thin and brittle-looking, her voice croakier than she recalled. She looked frail.

"Oh, how I missed you, my girl," she replied, reaching down to gently touch two fingers to Aelia's cheek. It was a strangely touching gesture, one she'd never made before. "Or should I say woman? I am so sorry I could not make it last season."

"The important thing is that you are here now. And I will not let you go so easily this time," Aelia said, holding on to her hand a few moments longer than necessary as she handed her the loaf.

"Oh, don't worry, my dear, I think I will have to stay here for a while," Lady Leda told Aelia with a smile, as she climbed down from the carriage with painstaking care. "Back in Naples, I struck a deal with a weaver who decided to fabricate pillows, and now I have a full cart of them to sell. Can't leave here until they are all gone." She reached the ground and stretched her bent back with a grimace. "But what I need now is the public bathroom. Can you take care of my cart? Just leave it near the bakery, will you?"

Aelia took the reins of the donkey and, as Lady Leda tottered out of view in the crowded streets, led it toward the bakery.

As she was tying the reins to a post by the bakery's front door, her hands started shaking so much she couldn't finish the knot. Except it was not her hands that were shaking, but the entire city.

The shaking was followed by a deep roar, and hundreds of incredulous voices around her cried out and pointed to the sky. Clivius, his wife, and both his sons raced outside the shop, then stood still beside Aelia, looking up in complete disbelief. Mount Vesuvius had just erupted.

"Why is Vesuvius erupting now? I am still young!" Aelia shouted to her dad in English over the confusion on the streets.

"What?" Clivius replied, still staring at the sky in shock. "What are you talking about?"

"I know everything, dad. I've known for years. I read your hidden notes."

"I … I … didn't know how to tell you." Clive replied. He was still out of his mind in disbelief; he had gotten comfortable and missed the most important point about time travel – anything is possible.

"It doesn't matter now. None of us are going to die here. We will sort out the time paradoxes later; we need to flee right away. Isn't that what your colored papers said? That those who stayed died?" Aelia tugged sharply at his arm, hoping to bring his mind back to the present.

The only "historical document" Clivius had about Pompeii was a tourist pamphlet he'd shoved inside his backpack and forgotten about when he first arrived at the ruins site. Since discovering it in the past, he had read and reread it several times, but, while it was a dramatic example of marketing, the piece had little useful information. He knew the explosion occurred at noon, resulting in an immediate rain of ashes and pumice, which, based on the huge mushroom they were witnessing, would soon be upon them. Although many fled the city right away, lots of people did not take it seriously enough and stayed behind. Hours later, as the force of the explosion dissipated, the whole column of hot debris and poisonous gases came down in a powerful sweep, forevermore burying Pompeii and those who stayed back – including, he always thought, his aged daughter.

"Yes," he said, his eyes finally meeting his daughter's. "We need to get the hell out of here!"

"Not only us. All of them, too." Aelia pointed to the people on the street. "We must tell them they can't stay here!"

As she finished talking, minuscule pumice stones began raining on the city. At first small and light, the porous stone didn't seem to be an immediate danger. Then a fist-sized piece of hard rock crashed down onto the head of a nearby horse, crushing its cranium on the stone street. That's when the panic started.

Aelia, still holding the reins of Lady Leda's donkey, gazed upon the cart filled with pillows and remembered the old merchant. "Oh no! Lady Leda went to the public bathroom – I have to find her!" Aelia pushed the reins into her dad's hand and went after their friend.

As she walked around the cart, the rain of rocks increasing by the moment, she had an idea. "Dad! The pillows! Use the pillows!" Demonstrating, she grabbed two pillows and used them as a makeshift soft helm, covering her head while she darted toward the nearest public bathroom.

"I can't find her!" Aelia shouted through the chaos on the street, returning to the bakery a few minutes later.

"Help me here!" Clivius shouted back, ignoring Aelia's worry as he scrambled through the pillows on the cart. "We need to save as many people as possible. Go knock on doors and give them pillows." He threw some to her, then grabbed another bunch himself and jumped down to the street, giving them to anyone he passed.

Aelia followed, doing the same, but returned to the subject whenever she was close enough to Clivius to be heard. "We must find Lady Leda! She might be hurt!"

The clear summer sky was now completely obscured by an all-encompassing ash dome slowly and inevitably floating down over the city. The pumice hail was getting worse; the pillows were actually saving lives.

"We'll search later, but she's smart, she might already be gone," Clivius replied as they took another batch of pillows from the cart. "Besides, I need your help. Your mom and brothers are helping the slaves salvage what they can from our home and the bakery. They will leave immediately for Salerno in our carts. We'll follow on Lady Leda's cart, but we have to clear the room. None of that can be found in the future."

As soon as they finished distributing the pillows and alerting the neighbors, urging them to flee with tales of doom and death, they ran back to the house. As Aelia followed, Clivius jumped down the stairs to the cellar, unlocked the iron-laced door, and swung it wide.

Inside the securely locked room, sitting calmly on a chair, was Lady Leda. "Hello, Clivius. Aelia. We need to talk," she said, in perfect modern English.

Aelia jumped forward and hugged Lady Leda, relief overwhelming disbelief for the moment. "How?"

"It's obvious, isn't it? I'm a time traveler. But not one as famous as you." She gently pushed Aelia back so that she could look into her eyes. "I know it's a lot to process. But we are hard pressed right now, and I am no longer in my prime, so I will make a deal with both of you. While you pack everything – quickly – I will tell you what you need to know." She pointed to three large empty grain sacks laying on top of the table.

"Don't just look at me. Hurry up!" Lady Leda scolded, setting Clivius into motion. He and Aelia frantically unplugged wires, collected electronics, and disassembled the makeshift generator into smaller pieces. As they worked, Lady Leda continued, "Before I begin, a question for you, my old friend. Should I call you Clivius, or Clive?"

He stopped for an instant, a coil of bronze wire in his hands, and looked straight at Lady Leda. Then his eyes wandered around the room. He noticed Aelia, busy with packing, but also a half-eaten piece of bread sitting in a corner where his daughter used to spend hours dabbling with his smartphone. A smile crept onto his face. "Clivius. My name is Clivius."

"Very well. Clivius the baker it is." Lady Leda looked satisfied. "You know, I hear Rome is in need of good bread these days. But enough of that, it is time for my story. We did not meet, all those years ago, by coincidence, Clivius. And yes, I was speaking English to my donkey."

"I knew it!" he interrupted with gusto.

"My mission since then has been twofold: first, to prevent you from making too great an impact on the past, especially with the dissemination of future materials and knowledge. I've been paying you to keep that paper from being sold, you know. Second, I was to make sure you had everything you needed at your disposal to teach Aelia about the future."

Aelia stopped in the middle of tying off one of the already filled sacks. "Why me?"

"Because you, my dear, are going to be the best of us. The child of two times. You will be fundamental to keeping the time-space continuum intact because of your unique upbringing. As soon as you are properly trained, your mind will be able to stretch the logic of time physics in ways most of us would never even grasp. But even more important will be your innate compassion and understanding for less time-advanced cultures, an acute perception of anachronisms and paradoxes, and beyond all that," Lady Leda waved her hand around as another tremor shook the underground room, "your fearlessness."

"What do you mean trained? For what? By you?" Aelia stood transfixed, ignoring the sounds of the sky literally falling.

"See, that's what I am talking about. No, not me. While I do love you, I no longer have the energy to train you. In a few days, another time traveler will contact you, and all will be clear. You see, my mission is almost at an end." A stronger tremor shook them. "May I recommend we leave now? We can talk more on our way out of Pompeii. Will you help me, my dear?"

Aelia took the smallest sack in one hand and supported Lady Leda with the other, while Clivius took the two heavier ones. They climbed their way out of the cellar and into the bakery, where they loaded the cart, which had been tied inside the bakery to protect the donkey.

"It looks like the stone rain has gotten worse," Lady Leda said, removing a gem-inlaid, rectangular pendant from her neck. "By the way, this is called a Chrolorogium. May I have yours, Clivius? We might be able to avoid a very unpleasant stroll under falling stones."

Clivius, reluctantly, removed his own Chrolorogium and gave it to her.

"Thank you. Now, you two climb onto the cart, while I sort this out." Lady Leda fiddled rapidly with both devices. She turned knobs, rotated wheels, and pushed buttons, while father and daughter settled themselves on the cart. "Here," she said, handing one to Aelia, "I finished mine. Hold it for me while I fix your father's, will you?"

Aelia took the device with care, looking wonderingly at the dizzying movement of the now-working face.

"Oh, one more thing, my dear," Lady Leda asked

absentmindedly as she focused closely on the second device. "Can you just close that lid for me?" Aelia complied immediately.

"What? No! Stop!" Clivius shouted a moment too late, as they disappeared from inside the bakery.

Lady Leda looked at the inert Chrolorogium in her hand and calmly put it around her neck. Her mission was almost complete.

She poked around the bakery, now in a state of chaos, until she found some wine and a full loaf of freshly baked bread. Her favorite.

She climbed slowly onto one of the stone benches, and configured the time machine for a jump a few decades back, just a few blocks away, inside the male section of the public baths. She pinched a bit of bread from her loaf and wedged it between the lid and the body of the Chrolorogium, preventing it from closing.

She then crossed her legs and settled her aching joints, leaning back. She took a sip of wine, tore off a still-warm chunk of bread and chewed it slowly, savoring. Now all she had to do was wait.

Aelia, Clivius, and the donkey – along with the cart filled with anachronistic materials – blinked into existence on an abandoned side road a few miles southeast of Pompeii. It was later the same day.

They tried to make Lady Leda's Chrolorogium work to go back and rescue her, but just as before, it was completely dead. They witnessed from a distance the ire of Mount

Vesuvius finally burying Pompeii.

Almost a full day later, they found the rest of their family. They decided to head toward Rome.

During their travels north, Aelia's mother broke an interesting piece of news to the family. She was pregnant again, and according to the augury cast by the priestess of Apollo's temple, Aelia would soon have a baby sister.

Behind the Timestream

B'LITK THROWS ITSELF into the timestream, selflessly. It does not regret, but it does fear. Will it starve to death if it never grows hungry and thirsty again? Will its consciousness wither into nothingness if its body never ages another instant?

It pushes these time terrors aside; there is nothing it can do about it now. And, ironically, time is of the essence. B'litk only hopes its unorthodox and dangerous plan will work. Or maybe it has already worked?

B'litk free tumbles for hours (or is it centuries?), its mind racing backward to what will happen, when it sees the first of its elusive targets.

Once every rotation of its body in the timeless void, B'litk sees a small dot of light in its path. Far away, but assuredly in its trajectory. The plan will work – or is it working? The timestream is already confusing its perception.

B'litk fixes its sensory organs on the luminous speck and surfs for a few more minutes (or is it millennia?), until the white dot comes closer and more in focus. It perceives, as expected, that the white dot is actually a small white rectangle. And it's not purely white, but marred by black markings.

As the distance diminishes, B'litk sees the dot take shape and become a four-sided polygon. It also can see the blanched surface change, every so often. The black markings flip and are replaced with others, similar, but utterly different.

B'litk needs to time this properly: if it hits the rectangle at full force, it is finished. If it misses the rectangle, it is lost forever.

B'litk is finally at appendage's reach of possible deliverance. It puts all its energy into squirming its body. It is going to make it! At the last moment it realizes that it is moving too fast and will crash. It twists once more, barely dodging the bulk of the rectangle while stretching out its limbs. Success! B'litk latches itself to the white rectangle's borders. It gets a good grasp, but the timestream continues to rage on, and eventually it will get tired. It must act fast.

B'litk anxiously watches the flipping of the white marked with black. Now comes the hard part. Convincing.

"Hey! You! Help!" B'litk's words read on the page.

It waits.

Nothing happens.

It tries again.

"Hey! You! On the other side! Help!" B'litk's words read again on the page.

Nothing happens.

Whoever is on the other side of the rectangle might not be from an advanced species. Even worse, the being might be from one of those backwater linear-dimension realities, the ones that only know about time relativity and nothing else. That was always part of the risk. There was no time to choose proper targets. There is just one path now: to keep trying.

"Hey, you! Pay attention. I will try again. I am here, talking to you there. Or, more simply, what I am saying on this side is showing up to you as words." B'litk's words read once more on the page.

"Yes. You. The one reading these exact words," B'litk continues. "You just need, for a brief time, to think in $@^n$ dimensions. I am, right now, in a very precarious position in the timestream side of the rectangle, having a conversation with you, in whatever dimension you inhabit, on the other side of the rectangle. From your point of view, what is happening with me has actually already happened on your side, which is why you are seeing it already written on your side of the rectangle. Got it?"

B'litk has no way of knowing if whoever or whatever is on the other side of the rectangle has gotten it or not. Has the device registered only its communication attempts or also what it is doing? What about its thoughts? In any case, it is clearly not a two-way communication method. B'litk has no feedback at all. The only thing it can do is carry on and hope for the best.

"My name is B'litk and I broke time." Please bear with me, B'litk thinks.

"We are the guardians of the Timeshards. The Timeshards are crystals that keep the vibrational membrane of the different temporal dimensions in balance. Without them, the whole temporal multiverse is in danger of collapsing. And, as I have said, I broke one of them. I had to.

"Our species, despite eons of existence, still has not managed to teach sense to our younglings. I am not sure how it works in your dimension, but in ours, the cuter they are, the more dangerous it is to leave them alone. Well, I left some alone, and a group of them tampered with one of the Timeshards. They were about to be painfully hurt, possibly erased. I broke the Timeshard to save them.

"It is my duty to restore it ... and I could really use your help." B'litk's words, against all odds, continue to be read.

"I am able, in very subtle ways, to manipulate other dimensions. Nothing big, or flashy; just small things. Things like this. Things like what I did in other locations of this same rectangle you are now consuming.

"You see, there is only one thing that can restore a Timeshard: the focus of time dreamers. Time dreamers like you. That is my plan. To find time dreamers, across the timestream, while they are in the act of time dreaming, and ask them to dream with me of restoring the broken Timeshard." B'litk hopes its words convey its energy.

"All you need to do is to think, and to enjoy, and to dream about time."

B'litk is shaken by a powerful undercurrent from the timestream, and one of its appendages loses its grasp on the rectangle's border.

"I am out of time on this rectangle. I won't be able to hold on for much longer, and I need to save my strength – lots of others still to go. Not sure if I told you, but I can't really tell if you are still there. I can only hope."

Another of its appendages slips from the border.

"One last thing. If you do decide to help, I changed some small things on your side of the rectangle. I scattered some Timeshard words, which you might recognize in your dimension as precious stones and crystals, in the other time stories in this same rectangle. One word in each of the stories. If you want to help even more, which is a good excuse to keep time dreaming, just go and search for them. You can even gather them in the challenge I left you on the next page."

The flow of time finally catches up with B'litk and it can no longer hold on. With a feeling of having done its utmost, B'litk pushes toward the next dot of light, leaving one last message.

"Thank you. Thanks for helping. Thanks for dreaming."

B'litk's challenge:

"I am counting on you. Find the Timeshards, or gemstones. There is one in each story. Write them down below and then go help me."

down

1. Another Time
2. Time to Light
3. Time Cleaners
4. Only Time Will Tell
5. Wishful Timing
6. Wild Times
7. Time for Everything
8. Better Luck Next Time
9. Tempus Pompeius

Timely Story Notes

Another Time

I know we (writers or authors) are not supposed to have a favorite story. When asked, the correct answer is 'I love them all equally, because they are all my children.' That is exactly why "Another Time" is my favorite story in this book: children. Or more specifically, one of my actual children: Oliver.

He once came to my bed, on a regular weekend morning during his early teen years, and told me he'd had a very strange dream.

"I was inside this giant wall clock, that was laid down on a table, and this giant bird kept pecking at the glass to try and get to me."

That was enough to spark my own imagination, and I

immediately thought this would be a great story. I carried it in my heart as a little seed for many months before it flourished into the story you read.

Unfortunately, I could not find a way to put the bird in the story, but if you pay close attention, you'll notice there are mechanical birds in the second clock.

Time to Light

Since I was writing a book of short stories, I decided to explore what was already out there in several social media sites and groups dedicated to books. On Goodreads, I found a group dedicated to short story competitions. Every month the moderator would choose a theme, anyone could then write a short story, and the members would vote for the best one.

I looked for the open competition, and that is when I saw it. The theme was an image: An imposing lighthouse atop a cliff. I immediately knew I wanted to write about the lightkeeper, but not just any lightkeeper. Some quick research led me to the stories of Ida and Grace, and that is how Grida was born: an amalgamation of the names of those two great women and their dedication to saving lives and keeping the light on. I never submitted the short story to the contest.

Go to www.stanlei.com/timetolight for the lighthouse image that inspired me, and to learn more about the real-life heroes Grace and Ida.

Time Cleaners

This is an ode to the everyday men and women. It started as a satire of big corporations, and what it would be like if they discovered time travel. But it ended with the aspirations, fears, and deepest emotions of a couple of janitors, who had the boring job of cleaning up time travel messes left behind by more glamorous Time Agents. We've read many time travel stories about the adventures of action heroes and heroines, but we never get the story of what happens afterward. This is one of those stories.

I have one thing to confess, though. I almost cried when John died. I even wrote another version where he survived, because their passionate kiss exchanged enough DNA between him and Mary that the nanobots did not erase him. (I know, quite farfetched.)

Despite my best efforts, John had to be erased. Only then could Mary unlock her potential.

On another note, the assassination attempt against Margaret Thatcher and her cabinet was real, and full of interesting tidbits. If you want to know more, go to www.stanlei.com/timecleaners

Only Time Will Tell

From the beginning, I knew I wanted to write a very short story that was more metaphysical in nature; more specifically, a story that would anthropomorphize time itself. Inspired by Neil Gaiman's Endless, I wanted to create a pantheon of the physics forces as if they were entities. With that in the back of my mind, I was looking for some quotes from Stephen Hawking, when I came across the quote about time. I ran to my bookshelf and searched for my very old copy of *A Brief History of Time* and there the quote was.

This sparked the idea of how Time entered the pantheon of physics entities, as a Lord, and in doing so, changing time itself. You can see them at www.stanlei.com/onlytime

Wishful Timing

As I was preparing to be the Dungeon Master in my weekly game of Dungeons & Dragons (which I played remotely with a bunch of friends in Brazil), I had the idea to transport them to a world like Arabian Nights, full of deserts, oases, and djinns. That is when I thought it would be fun to have a story with magic replacing science as the time travel mechanism.

Naturally, I thought of a magical lamp and three wishes. But then realized that if I had three wishes, I would never ask to time travel (there are more pressing wishes to be wished for), and that is how the genie that can only grant trips came to life.

The story started as an honest question: where would I go if I had only three time travel trips? The research the character did was actually done by me, and you can check it out here: www.stanlei.com/wishfultiming

While searching for where in the past to go, the future became the only option. I am not sure, but if I ever find a magical lamp like that, my choices may be very similar to the ones the main character in this story makes.

Wild Times

This might be my oldest story. It first saw the light of day during a high school short story contest. Among thousands of students, it was chosen as the best one. It was very different from this latest incarnation, with the exception of the time cage and the destination to the time of the dinosaurs. The only other thing that survived to this version is the main character's name (despite being male in my original story). I originally "borrowed" Hal from one of my favorite super-heroes at the time, the Green Lantern, Hal Jordan (and it is total coincidence that my first born is named Jordan).

And it was the desire to keep the name, to honor my earlier story, that led to Hal 3.0's life conflicts. To know more about Bambiraptor go to www.stanlei.com/wildtimes

Time for Everything

This is another very personal story. I was raised as a devout protestant, going to church several times per week for all kinds of services, youth groups, prayer groups, etc.

And since my early days, I could not stop questioning everything that I was taught or have preached to me. And sometimes the answers I would get back were quite disappointing. Especially the ones involving "the mysteries of God," which basically would require a suspension of human logic against the unfathomable divine logic.

Nonetheless, the divine is an important part of my history, and I wanted my first book to touch on it somehow.

As I was walking around my neighborhood, thinking about the stories I would write for this book, the

Ecclesiastes' verse came to my mind and with it, my younger self's doubts and curiosities.

And I thought, it would be great if at least once, my questions were actually answered in a visible, audible, and tangible way. An exploration of possibilities, where choices can deeply influence how we experience our "times."

I encourage you to read chapter 3 of Ecclesiastes (I quoted the New International Version), which you can do here: www.stanlei.com/tfe and then come back and read the story again.

Better Luck Next Time

As one of my beta readers wrote to me, "I was raised on Star Trek." The challenge here was choosing which of the several episodes that dealt with time travel I was going to use to create my parody.

After some research, and quite a few hours re-watching beloved episodes, I settled on "Cause and Effect." (The similarities of the stardate in that episode and the spacedate in the short story are definitely not coincidental).

Despite being a Next Generation episode, I could not pass up the chance to bring in some characters from the Original Series. Even if I did change Spock's gender. Can you tell who is a parody of whom? What about other easter eggs from the episode? They are all here if you are curious: www.stanlei.com/blnt

Tempus Pompeius

Early on in the writing of this book, I asked my wife to give me ideas about interesting places in the past. She gave me a list of them, and amongst them was Pompeii. As a newly married couple, in our very first trip to Europe, we found ourselves in Italy. After seeing Rome, we decided to rent a car and visit Mount Vesuvius and the city of Pompeii.

If you've never been, I strongly recommend it. Walking over the dead streets of a millennia-old unburied city leaves quite a mark on you. But there is nothing like being face to face with the plaster casts of the dead.

I knew the story would be centered around one of the plaster casts. But I was a bit lost, until we started reviewing our family genetic heritage, which we got from one of those ancestry DNA tests. By seeing how my chromosomes were so similar to my daughter's, the idea popped into my mind. And then it poured out, almost as an adventure between myself and my daughter, Loren. And the 49.8% match? That's the exact actual amount my daughter has of my own genetic material.

One more quite interesting fact about this story, is that all the content Aelia found in Clive's cellphone and computer was actual content I had on my own devices. To write the story I put my devices in airplane mode, and browsed offline to see what I could or could not read, listen to, or watch. Obviously, there was much more, but the ones I wrote in the story? 100% true.

In www.stanlei.com/tempus you can explore more about genetics and Pompeii.

Behind the Timestream

I am totally in love with B'litk, but don't ask me where it came from. I have no idea.

This was one of those stories where I sat in front of a blank page and told myself: "Go Crazy."

I typed random letters and glyphs until I had what could pass for a weird name, "B'litk … ", and then wrote after it " … throws itself into the timestream … ." The rest was just B'litk whispering to me, telling me who it was and what it was doing in the timestream. And despite the fact that I do not have a picture of B'litk, or any member of its race, in my mind, I will always think of it as closely resembling a tardigrade.

I hope you found the Timeshards scattered in each of the nine previous stories, and continued your time journey. If not, there is still time. Go to www.stanlei.com/blitk

Acknowledgments

First book. Lots of acknowledgments. I really hope that I am not forgetting anyone important. (If I do, then I will really need a time machine.)

Aline Sasaki Bellan, my wife. Without her you would never have had the chance to read my stories. She was fundamental in encouraging, inspiring, and allowing me enough time and space to put my ideas on paper. She has always believed in me, and for some reason, still continues to do so.

My kids have also really helped, in more ways than I can count (check the story notes). Jordan, Oliver, and Loren are a limitless source of inspiration and fun.

My mom, Marta Bellan, and my dad, Nelson Bellan, were the ones who allowed me to be who I am today, both by encouraging and repressing me.

My little brother, Stener Bellan (who is not so little nowadays), has been a faithful companion, for years, on everything geek. He read the whole book and pushed me forward, with lots of helpful conversations about and around fantastic themes.

Alisa Brooks. Impossible to put in words what she means in my literary journey. Calling her my editor is almost an offense. She started as a writing coach/editor for another book (which is yet to be published), then became a writing partner, a business partner, and a dear friend. But most of all, she is a relentless cheerleader of my stories. Even when she hates them.

Iris Lee, my business partner in our dream of developing inspiring content, zealously read every word I wrote, saw every iteration of the cover, and brought lots of comments and insights important to the final version of everything.

At this point, I am absolutely sure I will need to borrow one of the time machines to come back and include some people I have surely forgotten, but let's carry on.

In the beta reader and cover critic category, I must make some quite important honors: Steve Carter, Marlos Marques, Mark Zamuner, Duda Guerra and PJ Pereira were instrumental in shaping the sometimes rough concepts into workable stories and graphics.

Gratitude to Marcelo Pero and Natacha Lorente for the amazing graphic work on the cover. These guys really worked hard through almost infinite iterations, and the end result they came up with is spectacular.

Leo Rapini deserves a paragraph to himself. He believed in me for years and has been one of my major supporters. Not only did he give feedback on the stories and cover, but also helped develop the assets for the whole marketing campaign.

To all my friends and family on Facebook, Twitter, Instagram, and LinkedIn, you have no idea how important it was to share stuff with you and hear words of encouragement and love. Eternal gratitude.

About the Author

Stanlei Bellan, like any respectable time traveler, has many stories to tell. In other timelines, Stanlei has been a physics professor, an engineering graduate, a start-up entrepreneur, and a winner of six Cannes Lions awards for his creative work in advertising and entertainment.

An immigrant from Brazil who was adopted by California, Stanlei is still learning how to bend time to fit his wife, two sons and a daughter, a cat, his business partners, and his many hobbies (like playing Dungeons & Dragons and uncovering fascinating historical facts).

Stanlei's writing is inspired by an unquenchable desire to transcend reality into fantasy.

You can chat with Stanlei on twitter at @stanlei or visit www.stanlei.com to get a FREE STORY!

Printed in Great Britain
by Amazon